"YOU AREN'T HAPPY, IT SEEMS . . ."

James McEwan leaned back in his swivel chair, regarding Molly for a long contemplative moment.

"And you believe you should be happy. You believe that, all evidence to the contrary, you deserve to be happy—an utterly shallow, vain, trivial-minded woman like yourself, admittedly attractive. You have hooked up with a man who, by your own testimony, loves you—which you understand you don't merit, and probably you're right—yet still, you aren't happy!" He begins to laugh. "Forgive me," he says, "it's just, you know, so funny."

Molly, transfixed, doesn't trust herself to speak. Has she really heard what, it seems, she has heard?

Desperate to escape, Molly feels a powerful physical attraction to this man, even as she loathes him. How is it possible!

LIVES OF THE TWINS

ROSAMOND SMITH

AVON BOOKS 🔺 NEW YORK

This book is a work of fiction. Names, characters, places and incidents either are the product of the author's imagination or are used fictitiously. Any resemblance to actual events or locales or persons, living or dead, is entirely coincidental.

AVON BOOKS
A division of
The Hearst Corporation
105 Madison Avenue
New York, New York 10016

Copyright © 1987 by The Ontario Review, Inc.
Published by arrangement with Simon & Schuster, Inc.
Library of Congress Catalog Card Number: 87-13969
ISBN: 0-380-70656-3

First Avon Books Printing: February 1989

AVON TRADEMARK REG. U.S. PAT. OFF. AND IN OTHER COUNTRIES, MARCA REGISTRADA, HECHO EN U.S.A.

Printed in the U.S.A.

K-R 10 9 8 7 6 5 4 3 2 1

—for Ron L., nowhere in these pages

PART
ONE

1 At this most significant of moments, preparing for bed in their jointly leased apartment on the seventh floor of the handsome new glass-and-poured-concrete Greenwood Towers, after a year, or has it been more, of passion, and indecision, and speculation, and hesitation, and—much, much more: the intricacies of romantic love resist transcription—at this most delicate and intimate of moments Molly Marks, to her distress, finds herself in the awkward position of having caught her lover Jonathan McEwan in a lie.

In an untruth, it might be said. But perhaps it is innocent, or, in any case, inadvertent? Jonathan had allowed Molly to believe he was an only child—the only child of retired, somewhat reclusive parents—but in fact he has a brother: a *twin brother.*

As he says, reluctantly, apologetically, "An identical twin brother."

Molly stares at Jonathan. She feels her heart trip in apprehension, or is it simple dread. Or—a curious kind of elation? "—identical twin *brother?*"

Jonathan explains quickly that he *is* sorry he hadn't gotten around to telling her before now. But he didn't think it was very important. "In any case," Jonathan says, not quite meeting Molly's eye, *"he* isn't very important in my life."

"I see," says Molly slowly. "Your brother isn't that important in your life."

"No more than I am in his."

Jonathan's face is flushed with a guilty interior heat; Molly understands that he is lying even now. Even now! And though

3

Molly Marks is shameless as a liar—of sorts: but only out of necessity—she is quite astonished at this transformation in her lover. Dr. Jonathan McEwan with his high standards of professional and personal integrity, his dislike of hypocrisy and sham—how is it possible he is lying? And why?

Unpracticed in subterfuge, Jonathan does it clumsily and resentfully. Yes, Molly Marks is quick to note, the man gives off an air, very nearly palpable, of resentment.

"His name is James," Jonathan says. "But I think I told you that—?"

"James?" says Molly. "No. You didn't tell me that."

Jonathan pauses as if this information were profound, or doubtful. ". . . As I said, we're not very close."

"I see," Molly says carefully. "You're not very close."

Molly is wondering why this, why now, on the first night of their move into the apartment they have rented together; on the first night of their new life together; when they are both exhausted, and exhilarated, by the weekend's strenuous effort—why Jonathan has chosen to bring the subject up at all. Clearly, it is an awkward subject. A mysterious subject. Molly is considering what to say ("We don't have to talk about it now, darling") when Jonathan says, "You'll want to meet him some day, I suppose . . ."

Molly thinks suddenly, I've already met him! But she says nothing. Molly Marks is a very pretty young woman who suspects at times she is a little too clever for her own good; too clever by half, as a former lover wryly noted. And Jonathan McEwan, whom she loves more than she has ever loved any man in her life, is not a man she wants to impress with her cleverness.

So she leans against him, lightly, playfully. Hiding her face against his chest. They are in their new apartment, alone together in their new bedroom, *their* bedroom and not hers, or his, and everything smells wonderfully of newness and innocence and it is past midnight and Molly can't bear to see the anguished look in her lover's face ("As I said—we're not very close") so she leans against him as she frequently does, childlike, instinctive, inviting him to embrace her. And so

Jonathan does; he has never failed to embrace her at such times, even if they have been quarreling.

(It is a gesture—or is it a tactic?—Molly Marks has cultivated that allows Jonathan McEwan, who is six feet three inches tall and weighs a little more than twice as much as Molly, to feel tenderly protective of her. A method of subtle coercion but Molly would give it another name; and Jonathan, though he is a psychotherapist, and a shrewd analyst of others' motivations, could have given it no name at all.)

As he frequently does at such times Jonathan closes his arms warmly around Molly and rests his cheek against the top of her head. He is upset, Molly thinks, and why? why *now?* She loves him and believes she knows him to the very tips of his fingers—or does she? Jonathan is a shy man, but sometimes provoked rather too easily to anger. He is a brilliant man, it's said, in his profession, but sometimes baffled by matters of a personal, one might say an intimate, sort. ("The more you analyze your motives regarding love, the less you understand them," Jonathan once told Molly in so serious and touching a voice Molly dared not laugh.) Jonathan loves her very much, Molly is certain, but perhaps he doesn't know her.

In a voice that startles, it's so harsh, plaintive, disruptive of what she'd hoped was their new mood, Jonathan says defensively, "He just isn't that important in my life any longer. As I'm not important in his." After a pause he says, "—James, I mean." As if Molly might not know what he is talking about!

She whispers, "I understand." And perhaps she does.

Outside, it has begun to rain; Molly shivers in Jonathan's embrace. She twines her fingers together behind Jonathan loving the feel of the man's warm smooth heated skin, *his* skin, and in a way *hers,* for they are lovers, and will probably marry soon; begin a family—soon. Jonathan has not spoken explicitly of marriage, nor has Molly, biding her time, but— soon. This is the man, Molly tells herself, of the many, too many, she has known.

Now, to break his mood, his alarming seriousness, Molly gives Jonathan a fierce little squeeze. Often, making love, in

the quicksilver minutes leading into love, Molly is rough,
playful, tomboyish, wiry—she likes to surprise and she likes
to be surprised, overcome, "mastered" it might be said—to
a degree. For such a petite young woman she's remarkably
strong. She made a powerful impression on Dr. Jonathan
McEwan when she first came into his office a year ago as his
patient (though "client" is the word Jonathan prefers), face
pale and seemingly free of makeup, and angelically com-
posed; dark wavy hair falling loose to her waist; appearing
seventeen years old instead of twenty-seven in tight-fitting
faded jeans and a little white ribbed cotton undershirt worn
with nothing beneath. Her handshake was a quick hard
squeeze and her upper arms were hard little plum-sized muscles. On her left arm near her shoulder where you would
expect to see a vaccination mark there was a miniature but
intricately detailed rose tattoo—scarlet rose, leaf-cluster,
thorns—at which Jonathan McEwan, Dr. McEwan to Molly
then, stared intermittently for much of that initial session. As
Molly left his office he couldn't resist asking, "That tattoo
on your arm, Miss Marks—it *is* real?" Molly lowered her
eyes shyly, though she was pleased. She'd already made her
decision, she thought, about Dr. Jonathan McEwan. "As real
as anything about me," she said.

As a small child Molly Marks sometimes frightened herself by spying on her father when he had no idea she was
doing so. When he believed himself alone. Sitting in his study
reading the newspaper before dinner, shoveling snow in the
driveway, standing at a window looking out at a bleak winter
afternoon diminished to dusk . . . Molly hid watching Mr.
Marks who might have been any man at such times, a
stranger, no one she knew and no one who knew her. That
was the truly frightening thing: that he would not know *her*.
The thought left her weak, chilled, tremulous, but it was also
a thought, she saw in retrospect, that must have excited her.
It was a thought to prepare her, in case, for the jarring im-
personality of the world, inhabited by men who often looked
at her avidly but without recognition.

So it seemed a nightmare confirmation of her childhood

fear that, one spring day, in Manhattan, she sighted Jonathan McEwan on the street—Jonathan who was by this time her lover, and no longer her therapist—and he seemed not to recognize her. She was in Manhattan for the day, an hour's drive from Lindesfarne, Connecticut, where she and Jonathan McEwan lived; she had not known that Jonathan was coming to the city too, and felt rather hurt. (They frequently made plans to come into the city but at the last minute something always seemed to interfere: a suicide attempt by a patient/client of Jonathan's; a paper for a conference he was still working on; a crisis—there were so many such crises!—in a friend's life.) It puzzled Molly that Jonathan hadn't told her he was coming in but he was frequently reticent about his personal life—indeed, about his past—and Molly understood she shouldn't appear overly inquisitive: it is a tactical error to give a man grounds for believing you are more anxious about him than he is about you.

And now Jonathan was crossing 57th Street slantwise in Molly's direction, Jonathan who was Molly's lover but who appeared not to see her, shaggy head lowered, hands deep in the pockets of his tweed sports coat in that way of his that stretched the fabric and made even new clothes appear old; he was wearing a tie that resembled one Molly had given him, a green-and-aqua paisley, but Molly hadn't seen those expensive Italian shoes before and it seemed to her that his hair—thick, graying, disheveled by the wind—was longer than she recalled. The absentminded head-on plunge of a walk was Jonathan's, and the way he held his shoulders, and when he happened to glance up at Molly she saw he was Jonathan even as he seemed—eerily, terrifyingly—not to be Jonathan. For he saw her, *must* have seen her (she was smiling, waving), but he made no response, gave no sign of recognition, or warmth. Just kept going.

She might have been invisible—Jonathan's gaze plowed right through her and took nothing in.

She called out, hesitantly, "Jonathan—?"

She even said, in a small baffled voice, "Jonathan, it's Molly—"

But he didn't turn.

But surely the man *was* Jonathan McEwan, who loved her, who professed to love her?—a man in his midthirties, tall, wide-shouldered, swarthy-skinned, with a heavy head, thick eyebrows, a beakish nose, hooded eyes that gave him a sleepy lapidary look, a look of antiquity?—a most unusual face, indeed. It was impossible that Molly would mistake another man for him.

This was one of the profound moments of Molly's life! Like the telephone call from her father with the news that her mother was dying . . . like the call from the Women's Crisis Center in Cambridge, Massachusetts, informing Molly Marks that, yes, her pregnancy test came out positive (which was erroneous, some fool had mixed up her urine sample with another girl's) . . . like the expression on a cousin's face when the girl blocked Molly's passage on a flight of stairs in high school and said, ''I hear you've been telling tales about me.'' (Which of course Molly Marks had.) She stood there on the curb staring after the man she loved and felt such shock it was as if something were opening in her brain—a bird's wide white terrifying wings, the onset of madness.

These things Molly Marks did not do: she did not run after her lover, or even follow him—though, afterward, she rather wished she'd done so; she did not allow her tears to spill over and ruin her carefully made-up face, but dabbed them away with a tissue; she did not confide in the friend whom she met for lunch at the Museum of Modern Art—an old friend, male, gay, exceedingly handsome, from Molly's Provincetown days—when he took her hands in his, and smiled at her, and looked her searchingly in the eyes, asking, ''Molly, are you a happy person these days?—I do hope so.''

None of these things Molly Marks did, but she was badly shaken. She wondered afterward: perhaps in the busy, distracting context of midtown Manhattan she had not in some way—neural, neurological?—existed for Jonathan McEwan. Perhaps he could only see her, or recognize her, in a familiar context? He was of course an absentminded man; much of his time was spent, simply, in thinking. She recalled one of those tricky cognition experiments in psychology in which the subject is shown flashing cards to be identified in wayward contexts and sequences. You end up, even if you are cautious, exposing yourself as—easily deceived.

She didn't want to think: perhaps she'd fantasized her love affair with Jonathan McEwan—the times they'd been together, the conversations, lovemaking—and that, on his side, he didn't know her at all. Not *her*.

In any case, when Molly unlocked the door to her apartment that evening the telephone was already ringing and it was Jonathan McEwan behaving as if nothing unusual had happened; he was asking, with just the proper degree of hope, doubt, anxiety, if he could see her that night, still? Or was it too late?

No, said Molly, evenly. Of course it wasn't too late.

Pragmatic Molly Marks decided: she must have mistaken another man, a stranger, for Jonathan. It's as simple as that. A McEwan relative, perhaps. A brother? (But Jonathan had no brothers, so far as she knew.) Or: she'd been so obsessed with him at that early time in their relationship, so fiercely hopeful of their sharing a future together, of her *not* having made another mistake, she'd confused him with a man who had not really resembled him at all—just as she sometimes saw, or seemed to see, people she thought of as "lost" to her (primarily her mother, dead now for seven years, but other deceased relatives too, and people from her remote past, close childhood friends she hadn't seen in years). When she'd traveled alone in Europe one summer after breaking up with a boyfriend Molly had been so lonely it seemed she was always seeing familiar faces . . . except of course they were not, up close. She wonders if there is a clinical term for this aberration, some sort of mild visual or mental hallucination? Or isn't it mild?

Molly never tells Jonathan about the incident in Manhattan, not even by way of transforming it into one of her amusing little anecdotes. She has a keen sense of a man's—any man's—ego: a delicate thing, like something skinned and quivering in your hand, the tiny veins exposed. And though Jonathan McEwan is modest and sweet-natured and possessed of a healthy sense of humor she doesn't want him to be offended, even fleetingly, by Molly's having mistaken an-

other man for him. Surely there is only one Jonathan Mc-
Ewan . . . just as there is, Molly thinks, only one Molly
Marks.

Allowing even for her love, her infatuation, Molly is certain that Jonathan *is* an exceptional man. His idealism amazes
her. His old-fashioned zeal. He's a saint, in a way—so people
tell her. (But he works too hard, "gives of himself" too readily.) He believes passionately in his profession—in the therapist's ability to help troubled people—but his first principle
is that men and women carry within them not only the seeds
of mental health but the seeds of what he calls true creativity;
perhaps even—allowing for the vagaries of environment and
chance—greatness. He believes not in the natural trajectory
toward melancholia, resignation, stoicism so beloved of Freud
and his followers but in the mind's natural capacity for health,
even happiness. And for the acknowledgment of health as a
rational ideal.

What is called "neurosis" is therefore the consequence,
primarily, of irrational thinking. Even the most selfish person
is unconsciously striving to see the world apart from his own
use of it. ("I am?" Molly wondered, when Jonathan first
assured her this was so. "*I* am?") He'd told her that emotional and spiritual salvation had to do with this insight, this
revelation: that the world—other people, the very universe—
exist quite apart from even our perceptions of them: " 'Psychological' after all is merely a rather cold clinical term for
'Psyche'—soul." He spoke earnestly, passionately. An odd
way for a psychotherapist to speak, Molly would have
thought, but her eyes filled with tears, hearing such things.
Now that Jonathan McEwan is her lover and no longer her
therapist she hears them less often.

Molly Marks and Jonathan McEwan have leased a seventh-
floor apartment in a new high-rise building in Lindesfarne—
called by its developers Greenwood Towers and advertised
as a "luxury apartment dwelling," which perhaps it is. A
place of sleek but somewhat intimidating white walls, good
hardwood floors, an impressive kitchen and a tiny balcony
overlooking a miniature park. It is the first time in his

life, Jonathan says happily, and repeatedly, that he has ever lived with anyone. It's the first time he has truly been in love.

Molly buries her warm face in his chest. "Oh yes," she says. "Me too."

Jonathan has fewer clothes than Molly but they are heavy and bulky and take up a good deal of room in the bedroom closet. He has fewer books than Molly but they are nearly all hardcover books, many of them oversized, while Molly's are nearly all paperbacks, handily carried in shopping bags. The furniture is primarily Jonathan's because Molly's things were secondhand to begin with and she can't imagine them following her into her new life. Jonathan has brought with him— Molly insisted—his two pet box turtles which he'll keep in a tank of sorts in the second bedroom, his study; Molly decided it was most pragmatic to give away her pet cat St. Ives because Jonathan seems to be mildly allergic to cats. He has mysophobic tendencies, he tells Molly, and Molly is alarmed until she looks the word up in the dictionary.

The first time Jonathan showed Molly his box turtles she hadn't known how to respond. Box turtles are startlingly beautiful with their high-domed brilliantly colored shells but, still—*turtles?* These were *Terrapene carolina,* Jonathan said, he'd rescued them from a marshy area close by that was being bulldozed and intended to free them soon. As a boy he'd collected turtles of various species, tropical fish as well, but he hadn't much time for that sort of thing any longer. Molly bent over the turtles in their glass enclosure and wondered were the ugly creatures in their elegant shells unaware of her smiling scrutiny or were they snubbing her? She said, "Well—you can't get too attached to turtles, so you won't be heartbroken when one of them dies," laughing breathlessly though she suspected her joke wasn't really very funny, "—You might not even *know* when it dies." Jonathan was kind enough, gentlemanly enough, to let the remark pass in silence.

(Jonathan had explained to Molly some time before, when they were still psychotherapist and "client," that her compulsive witticisms, and the nervous laughter that invariably accompanied them, were commonplace signs of anxiety, which it was best for others to ignore.)

The decision for Molly Marks and Jonathan McEwan to live together in a newly acquired place, a neutral place it might be called, has been made after a good deal of deliberation—on Jonathan's side in particular. (Molly, in truth, would have moved in with Dr. McEwan after a shamelessly short period—shall we say two weeks? three?) Jonathan is, by all evidence, deeply and seriously in love with Molly but he is deeply and seriously absorbed in his work as well. Four days in private practice, a fifth given up to pro bono services at an inner city welfare clinic where most of his patients—and here they are, it seems, unmitigated "patients"—are impoverished black women and their children. "How do you do it?" Molly asked Jonathan shortly after they had become lovers, and Jonathan, staring at her, smiling as if in bewilderment, said, "Do what?—my job?"

Molly knows that there are men, and surely women, who become addicted to their own adrenaline: a fierce, even rather demonic love of work; a love of being in motion, perpetual motion, to the detriment, at times, of "personal" life. (Hadn't Molly been captivated by the experience of acting—at least during the run of a successful play?) She has no work she loves at the present time and so she envies her lover his energy, his perfectionism, the very strain of his work. And Jonathan is always working: thinking, calculating, brooding. Most of his private patients are young professionals with backgrounds similar to his own who define their main problem as an "obsessive craving to please" compounded by a "panicked confusion about who it is, or was, they want to please."

Molly warns Jonathan against being devoured alive by his patients; she warns him against burning himself out in their service. Jonathan, who resists being told what to do, answers curtly that the very concept of "burnout" is a cliché invented by people who never had anything burning inside them to begin with.

"I'm sorry," Molly says, her face smarting as if she'd been

slapped. She has just quit her fifth or sixth job in four years, for reasons of pride, and knows herself put in her place.

That weekend, as they move their things into the apartment, Molly begins to note that Jonathan is becoming, by degrees, unusually quiet—withdrawn. He *is* by nature a quiet man, a taciturn man you might say, and another word might be "saturnine" which is a word Molly likes but rarely uses in ordinary discourse: she isn't eager to show off her verbal intelligence. (She has discovered, though, that Jonathan was not born under the astrological sign of Saturn, for whatever that's worth. Not that Molly, a Gemini, believes in such superstitious nonsense.) Jonathan's patients talk about themselves endlessly, raking over the meagerly smouldering coals of their problems, failures, disappointments—like old-fashioned Roman Catholics gravely confessing, week after week, a perpetuity of tiny sins. To deal with them Dr. McEwan has cultivated a manner that is impassive, unjudging, objective, yet simultaneously alert and sympathetic: you glance up at him suddenly, as Molly recalls, eyes blurred with tears, and the dear man is likely to be staring at you, *his* eyes brimming with tears as well. Unless he behaved that way only with Molly Marks, with whom he fell in love.

Tonight Molly is keenly aware of Jonathan's shift in mood and keeps up her customary bright chatter, happy to be the leavening agent in their relationship whenever required and as frequently as required. She thinks of herself, still, as an actress, though it has been a while since she has acted—how long, she doesn't want to calculate. She'd been a model for a while too though not, as she usually doesn't explain, a fashion model. (An artist's and photographer's model. But only when she really needed the money.) Performing comes easily to Molly, easier, in fact, than being herself (whoever "herself" is). Since childhood, when she quite charmed her relatives, her mother's family in particular, Molly has been capable of cheerful amusing monologues that distract or seduce others even as she scarcely listens to them herself. She is skilled at gauging the effect her words have on others and rarely needs to pay attention to the words themselves. Once, she now recalls, she'd actually fantasized *she* had a twin—or *was* a twin—and that it was Molly's twin, not she, who performed while Molly herself stood at a little distance watching. It is important to listen not only to the audience's response but to the audience's silence, Molly knows.

She understands that Jonathan is beginning to be frightened of her. Not of her, perhaps, but of their being finally alone together in this new way—in this chastely new white-walled apartment. Always in the past, or nearly always, Jonathan would slip apologetically out of Molly's bed before dawn and go "home." And now he *is* home.

Jonathan uncorks a bottle of champagne and they stand out on their tiny balcony drinking toasts to each other between kisses. The night air is chilly for early summer, and bracing. How happy I am, Molly Marks thinks. How happy we are. A smell of wet leaves and earth, ripe rich things wonderfully romantic to Molly's way of thinking. She is reminded of, not other lovers and not love, or love's promise, itself, but of childhood: vague inchoate dreamlike memories. Being held, held tightly and warmly against the chill; nuzzling her face into her mother's lap or breast. I love you, she thinks. "I love you," she whispers aloud. Jonathan kisses her. "I love you too, Molly."

In the gleaming kitchen amid cartons of dishware they devour delicatessen food out of containers, and delicious food it is—they are both hungry, ravenous. Molly casts sidelong glances at Jonathan, admiring the man's severe profile, his dark-lashed eyes and heavy jaws with their underlying shadowy beard—a beard like shot embedded in the skin. She loves that air of his of intelligent solemnity—dignity—a melancholy (ancestral? racial?) that qualifies even his happiest moments. Even his most abandoned moments. Love for Molly Marks, particularly sexual ecstasy with her, would seem to be Jonathan's release; but only briefly. Fleetingly. Molly thinks of him as a man of weight, solidity, substance, depth; a man of texture. Unlike the men with whom she has sometimes been involved in the past. . . .

She has never been so happy in her life.

And perhaps it is the beginning, in fact, of a greater, un-
calculated happiness?

"I wish I could hold this moment forever," Molly tells
Jonathan.

"This? Now? With all these things to unpack in the morning?" Jonathan says.

"With all these things to unpack," Molly says.

It is that night as they prepare for bed that Jonathan tells
Molly about having a twin—being a twin. And Molly stares
at him astonished. Of course!

"His name is James."

Jonathan doesn't quite meet Molly's eye, as if he is confessing something shameful. He speaks in a slow, vague,
dragging voice Molly has never heard before—very different
from his normal voice with her, and from his professional
voice as Dr. McEwan. He is guilty about having misled her
and he is very worried, Molly sees, that she will want to be
introduced to his brother.

Of course he doesn't say this. He tells her that his parents
are retired, as he'd said, and are living in Arizona; but he
isn't an only child, he has a brother, an identical twin, a
"mirror-image" twin in fact, with whom he hasn't been very
close for the past fifteen years. When Molly asks why he
hasn't told her about his brother before he says he didn't think
it was important.

And it *isn't* important, he says, to him.

His tone is both apologetic and defensive. Molly continues
to stare at him, amazed. She sees again in her mind's eye
that other Jonathan as he'd materialized on the street—sees
again the way he merely glanced at her, unseeing, uninterested, as he passed her by. As if they didn't know each other
and were not lovers and of course they didn't know each
other, were not lovers. . . . Molly recalls speaking his name
as if it were a magic talisman that might make things right:
Jonathan. But the man's name was James.

She feels an instant's vertigo, as if, a second time, something terrifying were about to blossom in her brain. Jonathan
is looking at her now, waiting for her to speak. But all that

she might say under these circumstances, all that would seem to him ordinary, seems to her wrong. And though it is obviously the time to tell him that, quite by chance, the most unlikely of chances, she *has* seen his brother, she says nothing about this at all. "We don't have to talk about it," she tells him gently.

Jonathan, unclothed, is a bearish figure, not fat but solid, compact, covered in dark graying crinkly hair that grows most profusely on his chest and lower belly. He's fit but not muscular; hasn't time for exercise other than walks and occasional hikes, often at Molly's invitation. His massive head seems more in proportion to his body when he's undressed. His genitals, a rich blood-dark fruit, give the illusion of balancing his head. When barefoot he stands with his knees slightly apart and his toes flexing and digging into the carpet. A formidable presence, Molly thinks, feeling a touch of vertigo—excitement. When she embraces him, slipping her arms around his waist, she thinks, But this *is* James too!

When they make love—in Jonathan's bed, in sheets newly purchased by Molly—they are wordless as always, and more careful, more tender, than usual, as if solicitous of each other. And afterward they lie awake, listening to rain pelting against the windows, a sound distinctly different, Molly thinks, from the sound of rain in her old bedroom.

Jonathan lies beside Molly gripping her hand rather hard as if they were standing together in a formal pose, or positioned together, in state, as a bas relief on a tomb. His labored breath is slow to subside and he gives off more than his customary heat. He says he loves her and hopes to make her happy and is she angry with him?—for not having told her about his brother. Molly says of course she isn't angry with him. She loves him, she says, very much. Then there's silence and Molly feels suddenly a little drunk, giddy—the aftereffect of their lovemaking, the bottle of champagne. She grips her lover's thick damp hair and whispers in his ear, "Are you Tweedledum or Tweedledee?"—and there's an instant when Jonathan is shocked or offended but he laughs, snorts with laughter, a nervous relieved laughter.

"Tweedledee, I suppose," he says. "Since I was born second. And have always been what the trade calls the 'second' twin."

He speaks with such resentment that Molly knows she should change the subject. She assures him she doesn't expect him to tell her everything about himself and his family; she respects his privacy. "Only," she says lightly, "if you've been married before."

"*I* haven't," Jonathan says. With the suggestion that James has?

Molly wonders if her lover felt the obligation to tell her about his twin brother at this time because, beginning tonight, he and she will be living together in a simulation of marriage: they have become a definable couple, a unit. Perhaps he feels that Molly has displaced his brother in his life? Or that his twin might resent her? (But if the two men are not close—and they certainly don't seem to be—that seems unlikely.) He tells her that he and James had a falling out about ten years ago but that they hadn't been close for years before that, and even as boys, as very small children, they weren't close in the way people expect identical twins to be close. "Sharing the same genes," Jonathan says, "doesn't mean that we share anything else."

Molly asks hesitantly what James is like, and Jonathan shrugs in reply—"To tell the truth I haven't seen the man in ten years. I haven't spoken with him in almost that long."

"What happened between you?—or don't you want to say?"

"I don't want to say."

Molly asks impulsively, "Is he a psychotherapist too?"

Jonathan says, "Is that a serious question, Molly, or one of your jokes?"

"A serious question," she says, hurt.

"No," he says. "I don't think so. I think it's one of your jokes."

He sits up abruptly and swings his legs out of bed. Molly thinks despairingly that her lover is about to go home—having forgotten where he is.

Jonathan gropes for his cigarettes in the dark. He lights

one up, goes to stand at the window, his back to Molly. The
rain continues unabated. It is past two in the morning. Molly
says, "You'd better come back and get some sleep," feeling
wifely, chiding. Feeling just mildly alarmed.

She says, "I'm sorry if I offended you. It was a sponta-
neous question I think anyone might have asked but I'm really
not interested in your brother . . . any more than I would be,
I mean, if he were just your brother, and not your twin. Why
don't you come back to bed?"

"In fact he *is* a psychotherapist," Jonathan says. "He decided to train for psychotherapy after he'd drifted around and
failed at other things—it was a mockery of *me*. When we
were growing up he was always the dominant twin—to use
the clinical parlance—and I was presumably the submissive
twin but I always had the conviction, even as a child of two
or three, that I was allowing him to dominate, in matters I
didn't consider crucial. It was somehow within my power to
allow him—at school, for instance. He worked to exert himself as a presence, a popular presence, in a way I couldn't be
bothered to. He has always cared about being liked, having
influence, having friends of a certain rank—you know the
type." Jonathan was speaking quickly, heatedly. "Our parents made the mistake of sending us to the same school."

Molly turns on the bedside lamp and sits up, drawing the
bedclothes up around her. She's so small, forlorn, hair in her
face and expression so sweetly appealing—she knows precisely how she looks—but Jonathan doesn't notice. He says,
"I shouldn't have brought the subject up tonight. It isn't your
fault of course—it's mine. Your question is perfectly reasonable and I'm not justified in taking offense." And then after
a pause, "But people have such absurd notions about twins!
That we're 'psychically' connected, for instance. That each
of us knows the other's mind—that sort of garbage. It may
have been true in a very limited sense, in infancy and early
childhood—I don't remember this but people said we'd suck
each other's thumb in the crib, take turns crying for Mother,
invented some sort of baby talk together that no one else
        understand—but it seems to me that any two children,
        so much, developing at the same rate, in exactly the

same environment, would behave like that. And in any case I don't remember it.''

Molly listens, her heart beating quickly. She suspects she may be hearing things Jonathan will regret telling her afterward but she listens just the same. It's the late hour, the exhaustion of moving, the champagne, the lovemaking, the rain—she stares avidly at her lover as he paces about, naked, with no more self-consciousness than if he were alone. Molly has never heard him speak at such length about himself nor has she ever seen him so distraught. He asks her if she knows what is meant by mirror-image twins and she says no, not really, only what she might imagine: "If the two of you stand side by side you look as if you're mirroring each other?''

"If we stand side by side our faces appear slightly dissimilar,'' says Jonathan, ''but if one of us is viewed in a mirror while the other stands beside him facing the observer you can see that our faces are very nearly the same.'' Jonathan pauses. He adds, ''Of course, *we* can tell the difference.''

Molly laughs. But perhaps he didn't mean to be funny?

He looks at her, smiling quizzically. He says, ''But I haven't seen James in a long time. My parents say they haven't seen him either. He might look very different now.''

"Where does he live?'' Molly asks carefully.

''. . . I'm left-handed, as you know,'' Jonathan says, as if he hadn't heard, ''and James is right-handed. Our hair whorls in opposite directions. He used to get cavities on the left side of his jaw while I got them on the right. The vision in his left eye is a little weaker than in his right and the opposite is true for me. The summer we were ten years old I fractured my right ankle in a bicycle accident and a few weeks later he fell off his bicycle and fractured his left ankle. Of course, that was an accident. I mean—accidents.''

"Of course,'' Molly says, smiling. But again he hasn't meant to be funny.

"There have been a number of similar coincidences in our life,'' says Jonathan, ''—I mean our lives. But they're equally minor. They mean nothing. It's probably the case that James and I have less in common than ordinary brothers but since we were born twins other people expect us to be alike—

there's that tendency toward exaggeration, mythmaking. People like to romanticize twins, particularly identical twins, because they have the same genes. But—"

"Wait," says Molly. "What does that mean, exactly? To have the same genes—"

"How do I know what it means!" Jonathan says with an irritable laugh. "There's a sense in which it's all mysterious. Geneticists will admit they really don't know what the genetic code—DNA—is; they only know that there's something there, a process, an unfolding. On its most primary levels science is metaphorical—poetic. Like physicists confronting the atom and the parts of the atom and the parts that constitute the parts of the atom. And astrophysicists confronting the universe or the universes—all that *is*. You wonder finally what you are dealing with and if it can possibly be assimilated into a vision of the world that's sane."

Molly, shivering, thinks, Oh yes.

After this Jonathan stubs out his cigarette and returns to bed. His angry exhilaration has abruptly subsided; his skin feels clammy; he's quite clearly exhausted. He says, as if Molly were arguing with him, "I will never forgive James— no one can expect it. If they knew what he did, what he involved me in—"

"Please," says Molly, beginning to be frightened. "I don't think you should talk about this anymore tonight."

"I don't want to talk about it anymore at *all*," Jonathan says.

Within minutes he's asleep. For which Molly is supremely grateful.

And the next day, and the next, and all the days following, Jonathan never brings up the subject of James again. And Molly has no intention of asking him.

2 It is early September and Molly Marks, though idyllically if sometimes uneasily happy in her new life—she is not only living with Jonathan McEwan, she has begun work with a small public relations firm in Lindesfarne—is preparing to make a mistake half knowing it *is* a mistake yet unable to guess at its magnitude and what it will mean in her life. She thinks, It won't harm anyone. She thinks, Who could it harm?—Jonathan will never know.

She dials the number she has written on a slip of paper and listens with mounting excitement to the ringing at the other end. She half expects a man's voice and is startled when a woman answers and says pleasantly, "Dr. McEwan's office, who is calling please?" Molly hesitates and says, "I—I'm not a patient of Dr. McEwan's, I mean not yet—I've been referred to him—" "Yes," says the woman, still pleasantly, "what is your name? And who referred you to him?"

Molly wonders if she should hang up quickly.

She says, "My name is Holly Hawkes," in a stronger voice, "and I'm afraid I haven't actually been referred to Dr. McEwan in the most technical sense of the word. It was suggested by a friend that I make an appointment with him—"

"And what is the friend's name?" the woman asked.

"He wasn't a friend precisely, more of an acquaintance," Molly says, "—I think his name was Herschman, Hershberg—"

The woman is still pleasant; sympathetic. She says, "And how would you characterize your problem, Miss Hawkes?"

Molly thinks. Molly thinks hard. She recalls the sensation

21

she used to have—vertiginous, exhilarating, sick-dread spiced with glee, elation, euphoria!—when preparing to dive off a high diving board. (As a teenager Molly had been quite a good diver—she'd had visions of herself as Olympic-team quality but of course she hadn't worked hard enough, or cared enough, to get anywhere near that level of performance.) She feels that sensation now and realizes it is what has been missing from her life for a long time.

"Problem?—I have too many to characterize," she says.

The receptionist doesn't respond to her joke so Molly thinks quickly, of course it *isn't* a joke.

She says, half-shutting her eyes, poised, on her toes, "I was hoping Dr. McEwan might help me with that sort of thing," pushing her way forward, running agile as a dancer to the end of the board and springing up, out, down.

James McEwan is a busy man, evidently, like his brother Jonathan: Holly Hawkes can't get an appointment with him for three weeks.

Which will give me time to change my mind about seeing him at all, Molly thinks.

Molly Marks!—trailing her past behind her like her own hair braided stiff and heavy as an animal's tail.

She thinks of herself in the present tense as a way of not thinking about herself in the past. She is too young, she thinks, or should be too young, to have a past.

She has never had an abortion—thank God: it's so commonplace these days and Molly dreads being, or especially seeming, common. She has never had a baby or a miscarriage or been married or divorced nor has she lost any close, dear friend or lover she wasn't, virtually from the very first, prepared to lose. (Molly Marks prides herself on walking away first. Sometimes it's a sprint!) Nor has she had any serious illness—though from time to time she has been, as she told Jonathan McEwan and will, for symmetry's sake, tell James McEwan, "clinically depressed." But not—not *her*—suicidal.

"I would never do anything desperate," Molly says carefully. "I am not a desperate person."

It seems that Molly has no official college degree though she has attended enough colleges, universities, schools, academies, et al., in the Northeast, New York City, and California, as to have earned Ph.D.'s in several subjects. (Jonathan is under the impression that she has a B.A. in English literature and art history from Radcliffe, or is it Wellesley?) Sharp-witted and energetic and ambitious, Molly has worked at a variety of jobs since the age of nineteen—actress (both amateur and professional), model (both artist's and photographer's), Girl Friday for a half-dozen people in the entertainment world (including a controversial filmmaker, since dead by cocaine overdose, in whose *ménage* she acquired the exquisite little rose tattoo on her upper arm). She has done freelance interviews for *Vogue, Psychology Today, TV Guide, Runner's World, Gourmet, Ms., Architectural Forum, SoHo News;* she has been a stringer for the *New York Times.* She has worked for a Nautilus fitness center, for CBS television, for a private detective, for a funeral home. Now nearly twenty-eight years old she is waiting, still, for her life's vocation to declare itself.

She left her parents' home in suburban Philadelphia aged eighteen and since then has lived, of course, in a number of places. Sometimes, to amuse herself, or to terrify, she tries to recall them in chronological order. She makes no effort to recall the men with whom she was involved, casually or otherwise. Why did you come to Lindesfarne to live, Jonathan McEwan asked when they were first becoming acquainted, and Molly said jokingly, "Because I'd never lived here before and have no disagreeable associations."

It was in a gynecologist's office, sitting shivering at the end of an examining table in a paper smock and waiting for the doctor to examine her, that Molly had the experience—if "experience" isn't too extreme a term—that led her to Jonathan McEwan, and to what has been until now the happiest time of her life.

She was waiting, trying to think of nothing in particular,

trying *not* to anticipate the examination itself (a routine Pap smear—overdue by two years), when she happened to notice rows of snapshots, most of them Polaroids, on the wall beside the table. Snapshots of mothers with their newly born babies—there must have been fifty such snapshots!—and in some of them the doctor, a woman of hearty middle-age, was pictured with the mother and infant. Everyone was smiling, smiling. Happy pictures of new mothers and new babies and you would think, thought Molly, her eyes filling with unreasoned tears, that the world *was* a happy place. And there was nothing else you could say about it that had any genuine weight or significance.

While she was being examined Molly began to cry in earnest and when the gynecologist asked was she hurting her Molly shook her head from side to side and said, "Probably not enough." Later, sitting up, drying her eyes, she said laughingly that she had these spells, these moods, from time to time; usually at awkward times. At very awkward times! She waited for the woman doctor to smile with her but the woman didn't smile. She asked Molly if something was wrong and Molly shrugged and said, "I'd be the last to know," but that sounded too flippant, so she said, "Yes I suppose so—will you recommend a psychotherapist for me? I think it's time."

So she went to Dr. Jonathan McEwan, twenty minutes late for her first appointment and wearing one of her poor-girl/bad-girl outfits—jeans, boy's undershirt, expensive sandals long past their prime. She wore gold studs in her ears, a gold chain around her neck, and, yes, the tattoo which was real—indelible in fact. She had to flaunt the silly little tattoo as a way of not being ashamed of it.

Just as she had to flaunt her cameo-pretty face, her long hair, small-boned wrists and ankles. When others looked upon her admiringly or enviously Molly Marks was free to think, Then I *do* exist—it isn't a delusion.

A remark of Simone Weil's came to mind—"Every time I think of Christ's crucifixion, I commit the sin of envy."

She liked Dr. McEwan's office immediately. It was on the ground floor of a renovated Victorian house, a place of high ceilings, narrow windows, carpeted floors that creaked just perceptibly underfoot, a smell indefinable but comforting as of old wood, leatherbound books. Too restless to leaf through magazines in the waiting room, or even to remain seated in one chair for more than a minute, Molly busied herself studying the numerous plants arranged against a bay window: African violets, ivy, spider plants, a large fern resplendent as a peacock's fanned tail. She'd tried keeping plants from time to time in her life but they always died; it was like her luck—her poor luck—with pets. Dr. McEwan's plants were thriving but here and there were tiny shriveled leaves to be pinched neatly off. Molly crumbled earth between her fingers, liking the smell. Dirt lodged beneath her long nails but she scarcely noticed.

That morning, she had scrubbed her face hard; had put on no makeup, as if out of defiance. Defiance for what, or whom, she didn't know.

She was to fall in love with Jonathan McEwan after only a few sessions. Was this "transference"?—the mysterious but presumably therapeutic phenomenon of which Freud and others wrote with such obvious relish? When she first shook his hand she felt a weakness in her bones. Yes, she thought, him: this is the one. Aloud she spoke in her quick detached voice saying immediately—because she wanted it said—that her visit to him was purely experimental; she didn't know whether she would come back a second time, or even stay for the full session that day.

"Of course," Dr. McEwan said. "We're both entirely free agents."

That first hour Molly Marks talked about herself with clinical indifference, sighing frequently as if bored. Her recitation of her problems—that she was lonely but seemed always to want to be alone; that she worried she was incapable of loving another person, and unworthy of being loved in return; that her dead mother watched her, judged her, was not particularly happy with her, and so on, and so forth—struck her own ear as remarkably self-pitying and trivial. "I cry sometimes but for no good reason," Molly said, not meeting Dr. McEwan's eye. "I mean—there *are* legitimate reasons to cry but I rarely cry about them. I've even had the thought, more than once, 'I hope so-and-so doesn't die—I can't work up the energy to give a damn right now.' That's the kind of person I am; the depth of my soul."

"At least you understand that you have a soul," Dr. McEwan said. "We can work from there."

Molly, who had rarely heard anyone speak without irony of the soul, squinted over at him to see if he was serious. Afterward she was to think she'd never encountered anyone quite so serious—so intelligently serious—as McEwan. Anyone his age, that is. Older people after all haven't much choice about being serious.

McEwan was not a handsome man, Molly thought critically, but he had a decided presence about him. He knew who he was and that inspired confidence even if it might be a false confidence. He had deep-set eyes of no discernible color, the ghostly scrim of a beard about his heavy jaws, thick springy graying dark hair. Were it not for his name Molly would have supposed him Semitic. His conventional clothes—white shirt, tie, tweed coat badly stretched at the pockets—seemed inappropriate to his bearing.

His office was well-kept and tidy though lined with books; there was only one window, in which an ivy plant hung trailing glossy triangular leaves. On one wall was a vertical scroll in Chinese calligraphy, on another several photographs of what appeared to be exotic turtles' shells. A conspicuous piece of furniture was a large illuminated globe set on a mahogany pedestal. Molly wondered of what practical use was a globe of the world to a psychotherapist? She couldn't resist the urge to lean over and give it a spin—being a psychotherapist's patient granted her a certain degree of irresponsibility.

The world's continents were beautifully colored, etched into glass. Molly said, *"That's* impressive. *That* could make me cry."

Dr. McEwan, who had been staring at the little tattoo on Molly's arm, blinked at her as if she'd said something unusually perceptive.

Another conspicuous item of furniture in the office was a leather couch. An analyst's couch, evidently, though Jonathan

McEwan was not a psychoanalyst. Molly thought, I will never lie down *there*. She had too much pride, and a too highly developed sense of the absurd.

At the conclusion of the first session Molly told Jonathan McEwan she wasn't certain whether she wanted to continue—talking about herself like this, exposing herself, so to speak, to a stranger, was far more strenuous than she had anticipated. (She had thought it might be fun!) Fearing that her emotion would be too obvious Molly couldn't look the man full in the face. "I'm not sure I believe in this sort of thing," she said; and McEwan surprised her by laughing. "I'm not sure I do either," he said. "One-third of our patients seem to get well; one-third get a little, or even much, worse; one-third continue as they are for the rest of their lives." He walked Molly to the door, looming over her, slope-shouldered, rather graceless, smiling. "I sometimes think—though it isn't very professional to say so—that all men and women of intelligence and goodwill really know what it is they should do with their lives. Sometimes there's resistance, but beneath the resistance they know. The 'neurotic' is one who *works* at resisting."

In parting he asked her about her tattoo. Molly was stricken with both shyness and pleasure. This remarkable man had been attracted by such ordinary bait: *he was human just like Molly Marks.*

Of course Molly returned, Molly could not have failed to return. She had never been so powerfully attracted to any man in her life. Her meager psychological problems seemed to her precious attributes linking her to him; she would not have wanted to be cured too quickly—or at all. *I am meek but thou art strong* ran deliciously through her head.

In Jonathan McEwan's presence Molly maintained a certain degree of control (though she found it difficult to look into the man's face: her vision flooded with tears as if she were looking in too bright a light) but when she was apart from him she felt weak, petulant, obsessive. In one of her fantasies she knelt at the edge of his carpet, head bowed. "I am not worthy of your regard," she would confess, "even

your paid regard.'' Dr. McEwan would rise, startled, from
his seat. ''Please don't say such things, Miss Marks—Molly,''
he would protest, flushing with embarrassment. In another
fantasy Molly cried helplessly and Dr. McEwan had no choice
but to comfort her. No choice, no choice! He leaned awk-
wardly over her, embraced her . . . but even in her most
elaborate fantasies Molly could not force him to behave out
of character. He would make no sexual overtures to her while
she was his ''client'': he had too much integrity.

One afternoon when Molly had been seeing Jonathan
McEwan about three months she told him in some detail of
her mother's death. It had been the most profound experience
of her life—perhaps the only profound experience of her life—
yet sometimes, recalling it, and the funeral service, the cas-
ket, the cemetery, she felt overcome by a terrible hilarity.
Like wanting to sneeze; to smash something for good! ''I
saw that it was me, Molly—I mean it was *I*—who had died,''
she said bitterly. ''Part of me. The part she loved—the part
she took seriously. And I wished I had a sister who was like
me. A twin sister, maybe. Someone who was apart from me
yet *was* me, to preserve me. I've always thought that twins
must be very happy—identical twins in particular. Knowing
that they are doubled in the world. In a sense.'' Her voice
trailed off and she halfway expected Dr. McEwan to comment, as he frequently did when she digressed; but he said
nothing. She glanced at him and saw that he was staring at
her. But he said nothing. ''I didn't exactly appreciate my
mother when she was alive though I could see she was a good
person. I guess I just didn't care that much for *good* people—
they bored me when I was that age. Still do, I suppose. . . .
There's an American poet whose name I've forgotten, not
Robert Frost, not Emily Dickinson, I think it was—William
Carlos Williams?—in one of his poems he says that when
someone you love dies he takes a piece of the world with
him, the 'old life,' and that's the way it is. That's the way I
think of it in terms of my mother even now. My father's still
alive but he doesn't seem all that important to me. I feel that
my mother is still aware of me, knows my thoughts, knows
what I'm doing, or not doing, with my life. She's unhappy

about me but can't interfere. In dreams sometimes she appears—doesn't speak. Just stands there looking sad.'' Molly wiped her eyes and laughed, embarrassed. ''I don't know why I'm telling you such things, Dr. McEwan! I don't believe in an afterlife; some days, if I'm hung over, it's all I can manage to believe in *this* life.''

Molly looked up squinting at Jonathan McEwan and saw that he was still staring at her. His eyes were bright beneath their slumberous lids; he had not spoken in some time. Molly shifted restlessly, supposing he thought her a fool. When in fact he had fallen in love.

Before they became lovers in the most technical sense Jonathan insisted upon breaking off their professional relationship. He could no longer accept money from her, of course; he could no longer pretend objectivity about her. If she wanted, he would refer her to another psychotherapist whom he held in high regard. Molly told him she didn't need or want another psychotherapist—she was cured.

''*This* is the cure,'' she said happily.

Jonathan was doubtful. ''You shouldn't joke about such things, Molly,'' he said.

''I'm not joking,'' Molly protested, standing on tiptoe to kiss him. ''Don't *you* think I'm cured?''

Jonathan embraced her and lay his warm face against the top of her head. ''I never thought there was very much wrong with you in the first place,'' he said.

And now they are lovers; quite happily lovers; though Molly Marks is no longer quite so much in awe of Jonathan McEwan—nor is he, she guesses, of her. They have become, over a period of months, domesticated.

Molly thinks, I have never been so happy in my life.

Molly thinks, Never so at *peace*.

Why, then, does she plan to meet Jonathan's twin brother?—why, in such secrecy?

Why does she feel she *must* meet him?

Of course she did, in a sense, meet him once. Caught a

glimpse of him, at least. But this must be a formal meeting, a legitimate meeting. Though, in secrecy.

She understands of course that Jonathan, if he knew, would be hurt, puzzled, deeply angry with her; perhaps furious . . . unforgiving. Why, he would ask, why, *why?* . . . and Molly would have no answer.

Except: Jonathan had said he would never forgive his brother for some injury his brother had done but he had not said what the injury was, or in what way he was involved.

In his distraught state he'd spoken of complicity too, hadn't he. And ever after that night he has made no allusion to the subject, said nothing about his phantom brother though surely, Molly thinks, he hasn't forgotten. That emotional outburst of his—so unlike Jonathan McEwan.

It is a mystery; it rankles.

It *is* a mystery; and Molly must solve it.

3 It is on a warm September afternoon that Molly Marks drives to New York City to meet James McEwan; not as herself, of course, but as a neurotic young woman named Holly Hawkes. Since having made the appointment Molly half regrets having chosen that name—she half regrets having made the appointment itself—but there is no turning back now. Holly Hawkes, no less than Molly Marks, is not a young woman to retreat from an adventure.

The name Holly Hawkes is a trifle silly but there is a kind of logic to it: had Molly a twin, were she a twin, her parents might very well have named her and her sister Molly and Holly. Or Molly and Dolly. Molly and Polly? Parents of twins, particularly identical/single-sex twins, have long been notorious for giving their children cute names—Ronald and Donald, Tess and Bess, Annie and Fannie, Jimmy and Timmy; and much, much worse. As if the shock of having twins, two infants where one might reasonably have been expected, so throws them off balance they revert to infantilism themselves.

In the past several weeks Molly has been doing research into the phenomenon of twin-ness. She has found astonishing things, in some cases alarming things—one of them being that identical twins reared apart more closely resemble each other than twins raised in the same household!—for the reason that, when raised together, twins make a conscious effort to become individuals; there is something profoundly distasteful about being "identical" to another person. When twins are raised apart, however, without knowing each o

31

each naturally follows the bent of his instinct—the genetic trajectory of what might be called destiny. Consequently some of the twins in the studies Molly has been reading resemble each other to an uncanny degree: they unknowingly marry people with the same names, have children at approximately the same times and give them similar names; their I.Q.'s remain near-identical through life, despite differing environments, as well as their medical ailments; their tastes in food, clothing, jewelry et al. are remarkably similar, as are their personality traits and mannerisms. And of course they look alike. And are frequently mistaken for each other.

Fortunately, Molly thinks, Jonathan and his twin brother were raised in the same family, so they should be exempt from this peculiar sort of determinism. Though they have not communicated with each other in ten years they must have developed distinctly different personalities as children. Had not Jonathan said emphatically that sharing the same genes doesn't mean they share anything else . . . ?

Molly Marks finds it fascinating—and disturbing—to think that, had she an identical twin sister whom she didn't know, the sister would very likely resemble her to an uncanny degree. Each, believing herself a distinct individual, would turn out to be a mirror-image of the other. What a shock it would be to meet as adult women. . . . Might they even fall in love with the same man? Or men? Most of the twins in the research studies were reported to have married spouses who resembled each other.

There is a point, Molly thinks, at which contemplating such things is no longer fascinating—it's disturbing. Very disturbing.

The fictitious "Holly Hawkes" is to be Molly Marks in most details, of course. For scientific, experimental purposes Molly intends to duplicate her early experiences with Jonathan McEwan as closely as possible.

So she is wearing the very outfit she wore for her first session with Jonathan. Tight-fitting jeans, boy's white ribbed undershirt (with nothing beneath), the same pair of sandals in slightly worse condition. Gold studs, gold chain; hair falling lavishly down her back; tattoo prominent. Ah, her shameful little tattoo! Her delicious little tattoo! Molly examines herself in every mirror and mirrored surface she passes on her way to James McEwan's address and thinks, yes, she looks good today; she looks very good. Better, in fact, than she'd looked when she stepped into Jonathan McEwan's office many months before.

And why?—because Molly Marks is a much happier woman now than she was then. A woman is always more beautiful when she knows herself loved.

Dr. James McEwan, Psychotherapist, has his office on the ground floor of a handsome brownstone building on East 83rd Street, a half-block from Fifth Avenue. Molly is impressed by the neighborhood and by the brownstone—she judges that, as a psychotherapist, James McEwan has been quite successful. (Perhaps somewhat more successful than Jonathan?—but Jonathan happens to be a man to whom money means relatively little. Molly has discovered to her distress that a number of his clients owe him money and that he is reluctant to press them to pay even when he suspects them of bad faith.)

The brownstone is four stories high, with a cramped front yard surrounded by a spike-topped wrought-iron fence. A solitary ginkgo tree grows in the yard, amid patches of burnt-out grass; stunted geraniums grow in flowerpots someone has arranged perfunctorily on a window ledge. A large air conditioning unit is humming and vibrating in the window, dripping water. Molly checks her reflection a final time in her compact mirror and rings the buzzer.

"Jonathan is too good," she tells herself. "He would never hate me for this."

James McEwan's receptionist is a tall, gaunt, excessively smiling woman, a faded beauty Molly guesses, with that air, at once solicitous and aggressive, of the deeply resentful. The poor woman is probably in love with her employer—isn't it inevitable in such circumstances? (Though Jonathan McEwan's receptionist, a plain, plump, good-natured married

woman of middle age, is not obviously in love with him.) To
her relief Molly sees that James McEwan's waiting room is
considerably different from Jonathan's: it is less spacious,
and its furnishings are more strikingly contemporary; its at-
mosphere is darker—so little natural light comes through the
single front window that, even at midday of a sunny day,
artificial lights are burning. The walls are hung with primitive
African masks—or are they stylized versions of masks, very
nearly caricatures? Elongated O's for eyes; wide-gaping grins;
shocks of black hair coarse as a horse's tail. There are six
masks on the wall facing Molly and each is uglier than the
other. Here is a taste very different from Jonathan's!

Still, there is a plant, a single enormous fern, in the window. The most beautiful fern Molly has ever seen. Is it real?—
it's so perfect. Is it an ingenious imitation? Molly reaches
over stealthily to poke her fingers in the black dirt. The dirt
is real, but dry, as if it hasn't been watered in a very long
time. The fern itself is rather elastic to the touch.

Molly waits. For twenty very long minutes. She's nervous
as a cat, shivering from the air conditioning. Thinking, If I
walk out now no harm will have been done.

Thinking, If I walk out now I am still innocent.

What had intrigued her in the twin research studies was
the predilection of twins for the same spouses. Not always of
course but with a high degree of frequency. In one case study
a set of female twins fell in love with the same man, and
became lifelong enemies as a consequence. (The man married neither.) In another case study male twins had what was
virtually a single love affair, over a period of twenty-odd
years, with the same woman *while they were married to other
people*. Their defense of their behavior particularly struck
Molly: each twin said he couldn't help himself, it was "just
something that happened."

The telephone rings frequently in Dr. McEwan's office and
Molly hears the receptionist's smooth, pleasant, uninflected
voice without making out any of her words. No one else
comes in; if there is a patient with Dr. McEwan he or she
will probably leave by a side or rear door—that, at least, is
Jonathan's practice. When, finally, Molly is shown into James

McEwan's office she makes an effort to carry herself with as much studied nonchalance as when she'd entered Jonathan's office. It is like walking on stage!—like running forward and springing off the high board!—and she means to do it well.

She steels herself for the psychic shock of meeting a man who so resembles Jonathan yet isn't, for all her premeditation, prepared for it. Even as James McEwan smiles rather tightly at her, and reaches out to shake her hand, as Jonathan had done in the same gesture months ago, Molly stares at the man transfixed, her eyes opening wide in horror and her bowels clutching. It is impossible! she thinks. A quirk of nature! This man *is* Jonathan, surely?—whom she had kissed goodbye only a few hours before, with whom she'd made love the previous night?

He seems to recognize her too. His heavy-lidded eyes—how like a snake's hard eyes they are!—flare up for an instant in a look of unsettling intensity.

Molly tries to stammer a coherent greeting but she is losing control. She sways on her feet; her lips drain rapidly of blood; her slender fingers, in James McEwan's enormous fingers, are icy cold. She knows now she has made a terrible mistake but there is no escaping—the man is gripping her hand tight, painfully tight, as if to prevent her.

"Miss Hawkes?" he says. "Is something wrong?"

It is Jonathan's voice, but deeper; thickened. Less kind.

Molly tries to reply but cannot. She is going to faint—her legs give way beneath her—she would fall heavily to the floor if James McEwan were not there to prevent it.

Molly never really loses consciousness in James McEwan's office that day—or doesn't believe she does—but she must lie for five or more minutes on a couch (a couch in dark brown leather that resembles the one in Jonathan's office but is newer, probably more expensive) until she feels strong enough to sit in a chair by his desk. James doesn't seem particularly surprised at her behavior, nor does he call in the receptionist to give her aid, for which Molly is extremely grateful. What an entrance!—what a fool she has made of herself! Already the experiment, so-called, is botched.

The man is no taller, no bigger, than Jonathan; but he gives the impression of being so. He seems to take up more space. That massive shaggy head, eyebrows so thick as to appear snarled, darkly bright sleepy eyes—this *is* Jonathan—yet a Jonathan subtly altered. His movements are a little rougher, less studied. His manner is more relaxed. He is wearing a stylish sports coat in oyster-pale linen that resembles nothing of Jonathan's, and a shirt in a floral print, blues and greens, with no tie. His trousers, perfectly creased, are of a fine dove-gray fabric—not Jonathan's taste. Yet his wristwatch is Jonathan's—the very same watch. He holds his shoulders in the same way, and inclines his head in the same way, and his facial mannerisms—that frowning smile, or smiling frown, sharply bracketed by creases around the mouth—are Jonathan's. He even whistles thinly under his breath as Jonathan does, though Jonathan whistles only in completely relaxed moods, and would never behave so nonchalantly in the office. Jonathan would be shocked at such unprofessional, if not insulting, behavior.

It must mean that James is extremely popular with patients, Molly thinks resentfully. Her impression is that the man doesn't give a damn about her—she'll start the interview when she's ready and until that moment he doesn't want to waste time. He busies himself opening mail, even makes a telephone call—a conversation punctuated by laughter—without so much as an apologetic glance in Molly's direction.

Still, Molly finds it difficult throughout the entire interview, on an instinctive, perhaps purely physical, level, to believe that the man before her is a literal stranger to her. That they haven't made love; are not *in* love and intimately connected—profoundly, unthinkingly, connected. She tells herself that James McEwan is only Jonathan's brother, she can see there are significant differences between them, yet, the more she stares at him, the more she contemplates the fact of him, the more she thinks, against the very grain of reason, that, somehow, granted all these qualifications, the man *is* her lover.

And that he senses it too.

* * *

"Are you in the habit of fainting frequently, Miss Hawkes?"

"Of course not. Never."

"Except at certain selective times?"

"No," says Molly, feeling a stab of hurt. "Never."

Is he mocking her?—or is that look of his, like Jonathan's, gentle, kindly, probing?

"I have never fainted before in my life," Molly says stubbornly. "In fact I didn't faint now. I just felt weak."

Molly begins to speak with more confidence; as long as she doesn't look at James—his gaze is as unsettling as Jonathan's had been in the early stages of their acquaintance—she can perform more or less as she'd planned. She has only to imitate the Molly Marks of the past, the Molly who made so powerful an impression on Jonathan McEwan. (Though of course she isn't that young woman any longer—hasn't she been cured of her psychological ailments?)

James McEwan leans far back in his creaking swivel chair, hands clasped behind his head, a pose of almost insulting casualness but he is obviously caught up by her remarks—the familiar litany of a neurotic's ailments. He says nothing but he watches her intently, and respectfully, she thinks, nodding from time to time (a mannerism of Jonathan's in similar circumstances), staring at the flimsy cotton undershirt through which her small shadowy breasts define themselves, and her little rose tattoo. Molly swallows hard and tells herself, This should be easy! I've lived it all before!—feeling the unmistakable drift of a man's sexual interest.

Pretty Holly Hawkes, twenty-seven years old, never married, adrift, as she says, in life, believes that she needs psychotherapy after years of having resisted; she was referred to James McEwan by a friend of a friend. She is lonely—always lonely—even when she is with people she likes—or loves; she is living with a man at the present time whom she loves but—and here is the problem, the perennial problem!—she sometimes feels a terrible sense of loneliness even when she is with this man—a good, kindly, superior man; *even when they are making love.* "That can't be normal!" Molly says questioningly.

James McEwan, staring at her, nods absentmindedly but says nothing.

The recitation continues. Molly is a good actress but she speaks more rapidly than she intends—James's intense interest is disconcerting. She tells him about her irrational fear of her heart stopping—her worry that she is incapable of loving another person, and unworthy, herself, of being loved—her delusion that her dead mother is somehow watching her, judging her. And so on and so forth; though these problems belong to Holly Hawkes, and not to Molly, Molly feels her eyes smart with tears.

She looks around James McEwan's office as if half consciously seeking points of reference. It seems wrong to her eye that, in place of Jonathan's elegant Chinese scroll, there is a rather ugly copper shield, all surface, shining and featureless as a mirror. (Perhaps its function is to draw off the nervous intensity of the patient?—Molly steals surreptitious glances at herself in it.) On the wall directly behind James are several African masks, luridly painted, jeeringly ugly; and a half-dozen framed photographs, portraits of presumably distinguished men whose expressions mimic, perhaps accidentally, those of the masks—Molly recognizes Nietzsche, Freud, Gurdjieff, Nijinsky. (Each portrait has a caption but Molly can make out only the one for Nijinsky—"I am God, I am God!") There is no lovely illuminated glass globe beside James's desk, only an aluminum typing table stacked with journals and papers. On the floor are more journals, papers, books, sections of the *New York Times* strewn messily about; an ashtray heaped with ashes and cigarette wrappers; empty delicatessen containers stuffed with crumpled napkins. Molly stares at these, vaguely disturbed. Does James McEwan eat his lunch at his desk?—Jonathan's habit too, except on days when Molly drops by his office to take him out to lunch.

Molly brings Holly Hawkes's little speech to an end, rather weakly. She isn't certain, she says, that she believes in psychotherapy; she isn't certain she really wants to go through with it. "I hope you'll be frank with me . . ." she says.

James McEwan, still leaning back in his swivel chair, hands

behind his head, regards Molly for a long contemplative moment. Has he heard? Has he even been listening? His eyes are very like Jonathan's but harder, blacker; more deeply recessed. His skin appears to be darker too, a golden-olive tan, and his hair, thick, springy, streaked haphazardly with gray like Jonathan's, is worn an inch or so longer than Jonathan's. The strong blunt bones of James's face remind Molly of a skull.

He says curtly, "Of course I will be frank with you, Miss Hawkes. I am never less than frank; no one can bribe me not to be." He smiles at Molly, as if to soften the impact of his words. "Your problems are one single problem, my dear, a thoroughly commonplace one, and I *can* treat you—provided you concur with my mode of therapy, and don't offer the usual token resistance. It will be costly—I don't come cheap— but you should be cured, to the degree that a 'cure' is possible, within a few months."

Molly stares at the man, astonished. His tone is so supercilious, so smug! She has never heard anything quite like it in her life.

"You aren't happy, it seems," James continues, "—and you believe you should be happy. You believe that, all evidence to the contrary, you deserve to be happy—an utterly shallow, vain, trivial-minded woman like yourself, admittedly attractive but not so attractive as you might wish, and no longer really young. You have hooked up with a man who, by your own testimony, loves you—which you understand you don't merit, and probably you're right—yet, *still*, you aren't happy!" He begins to laugh, fairly snorting with laughter. It is Jonathan's most robust, abandoned, infectious laughter— exploding from James with such force that his eyes narrow to slits even as his nostrils, deep black O's in his face, widen like a horse's. "Forgive me," he says, wiping his eyes carelessly with the back of his hand. "It's just, you know, so *funny.*"

Molly, transfixed, doesn't trust herself to speak. Has she really heard what, it seems, she has heard?

James recovers from his laughing fit and says, more soberly, "Of course it is possible that I've misjudged you—the depth of your personality, that is. Women sometimes present themselves in the most asinine of ways, behaving like virtual morons, employing their charms in the dubious project of— *do* forgive me—seduction. The temptation is strongest for a good-looking woman, of course. I can understand that. I can even sympathize, to a degree.'' He smiles at Molly, who continues to look at him with an expression of utter disbelief. ''I suppose you've been successful along these lines, Miss Hawkes?—or may I call you Holly?—since about the age of sixteen?''

Molly gets shakily to her feet. ''I don't have to stay here and be insulted,'' she says.

''Well—that's your option; you'll be billed for the full hour in any case,'' James says agreeably.

''I don't have to stay here,'' Molly repeats, trembling with hurt and indignation, ''—and be insulted by an arrogant bastard like you!''

James laughs again. He gets to his feet as if to escort Molly from the room but, at the door, holds it shut, his hand over her head. He looms over her, amused, appreciative, playful, in a way protective; he draws his face rather close to hers. Molly shrinks from his warm meaty breath and feels her back hard against the door. ''My dear, as I said, I am willing to take you on as a client—a *client*, not a *patient*—if you like. There's an opening at this time: one of my less stable clients seems to have disappeared permanently,'' James says. ''Of course we'll have to discuss my fee. And whether you can afford it. And whether, you know, you're a serious woman— or a silly little twat. I don't on principle believe in treating certain people since to cure them of their 'vices' is to deprive them of the only interesting thing about them.''

Molly says, stammering, ''You're crazy. You!—you're crazy! You aren't a psychotherapist—how dare you call yourself a psychotherapist!''

''I *am* a psychotherapist,'' James says evenly, ''but I don't thrust myself on others. Take me or leave me; you're a free agent.''

Molly turns the doorknob, desperate to escape. She feels

a powerful physical attraction to this man, even as she loathes him, and is terrified he will attack her. How is it possible!

He closes his fingers around her bare upper arm and rubs at her tattoo with his thumb. "This real?" he asks, curious.

Molly slips out the door, Molly escapes. Afterward she will discover reddened marks in her flesh—the imprint of James McEwan's fingers.

4. "Is something wrong, Molly?" Jonathan asks. "You seem unusually distracted."

"Do I? —I'm not," Molly says.

Her answer is quick and defensive; edged with guilt.

"I don't mean to be," Molly says.

She looks up fearfully at Jonathan and sees him watching her with concern, love—*is* it love? She presses herself against him in a childlike plea for help.

That bastard, she thinks—that beast.

James, she means.

Him.

It is a week after Molly's adventure in New York City, or is it ten days—two weeks? She has been thinking about James McEwan obsessively since then: wishing she'd slapped his arrogant face. Or spat into it. Wishing she'd had some idea of what to expect from him so that she might have been more of a match for him.

Though, perhaps, Jonathan had suggested what the man was like, in essence. And Molly had had to see for herself.

Well, I've learned, Molly thinks.

Shallow, vain, trivial-minded. Asinine. Moron. Silly little twat. The man's frank, flat, bemused voice: not even a voice of mockery or cruelty. Just truth-telling.

Hadn't he said he could not be bribed to be anything other than frank?

I've learned, Molly thinks. She is bitter, incensed, aroused as if for battle, even now. Even in Jonathan's arms. His big body protecting her small wiry nerved-up body and Molly is

42

thinking even now of *him*, hearing *his* voice, feeling *his* fingers closing about her bare arm.

"Are you worried about something?" Jonathan asks uneasily. "Is it your work?"

"No," says Molly, not quite hearing the question. She presses herself against Jonathan so that he can't see her face. "—Yes, I suppose it is."

"You're always telling me that I work too hard, that I'm exhausting myself," Jonathan says. "And now you're doing the same thing."

"Oh not the same thing, surely!" Molly says with a wan little laugh.

And later that evening, preparing for dinner, when Molly lights the candles on the table she stands for so long, distracted, holding a lighted match to a badly bent candlewick that won't take the flame, that she burns her fingers and drops the flaming match onto the table. Jonathan says sharply, "Molly. For Christ's sake. You look as if you're asleep on your feet."

And is it that same evening, or another, similar evening, in mid-October, Molly tells Jonathan as they are undressing for bed that she wants to have a baby . . . if she is going to have a baby . . . before she is thirty years old. And Jonathan hesitates perceptibly as of course she knew he would (just as Molly would have hesitated had Jonathan been the one to make the declaration) and Molly bursts into tears and says, "You don't love me, then! That's obvious! You don't love me enough!"

She says, "I really don't know what's wrong with me lately—I thought I was cured of the problems I had when I was your patient."

Jonathan corrects her automatically: "Client."

"*Client,*" Molly says. "Yes. Except, you know, some people are *patients*—aren't they?"

"Those are only linguistic conventions," Jonathan says stiffly. He is always rather defensive when questioned about his professional practice. It means so much to him; he takes it so very seriously; he's priestly, Molly thinks, rabbinical—oddly, like his brother. The one so somber in his vocation, the other so seemingly casual. But they look like the real thing: that face, those eyes, the air of authority. You just naturally want to fall down on your knees on the carpet, Molly thinks ironically. Oh yes!

". . . only conventions," Jonathan says. "Deriving from an outdated medical model, a biological model."

"They're conventions rooted in fact, don't you think?" Molly persists. In recent weeks she has been quick to quarrel with Jonathan over small matters, like this; as if she wants to impress him with her intellectual acuity. She *is* after all an intelligent woman.

Jonathan says, "Psychotherapy should be as close to a relationship between equals as possible—both the therapist and the client involved in a search for the resolution of the client's problem. I really detest the old Freudian model—I am a psychotherapist but I don't impose myself on others: my clients are free agents, it's as simple as that. Of course, as you know, I rarely treat psychotics—they're in a different category. I suppose I treat men and women rather like myself, with whom I can identify."

"You're hardly an equal with your clients, Jonathan," Molly says. She speaks quickly impatiently, with no intention of flattering. "You're superior—you are a superior man. No, don't look embarrassed, or annoyed—please. It's true. Otherwise why would they, why would we, come to you? Why would we pay you?"

"I think of myself as a helper, an expert of a kind in an area of life others don't know as much about because they haven't explored it," Jonathan protests. "Not a tin god. Not a guru. I *hate* that sort of smug elitism—the therapist who abuses his role by bullying his clients, imposing his will upon them, speaking glibly of 'cures.' As if there can be a 'cure' for the soul's yearnings. . . . The worst sort of therapist is the one who acts out his sado-aggressive fantasies with his clients. It's too easy, for one thing, like molesting children. It's contemptible."

Molly says, as if impulsively, "Your brother—what kind of psychotherapist is he?"

"My brother . . . ? Why do you ask about him?" Jonathan says, surprised. Molly has offended him but he will try to disguise it. He says quickly, "I don't know about him. His principles, or his practice. Sorry."

"I was just wondering if he shares—shared?—your ideas," Molly says weakly. "I realize you haven't seen him in a long time—"

"I doubt it that he shares any of my ideas," Jonathan says. "I really don't know."

"You went through the same professional training, didn't you?" Molly asks.

Jonathan looks at her. "Who told you that? Did I tell you that?"

"Didn't you?"

"I don't remember telling you about it—when did I tell you?"

"A while ago. A few months ago. The night we moved into the apartment."

"Yes, I remember that," Jonathan says with distaste. "I was drunk that night. I remember saying things that were ill-considered and perhaps even inaccurate and I was hoping you might have made allowances for me and not taken it too seriously. That you wouldn't have hoarded bits of information to use against me at a later time."

Molly looks at him astonished. "Hoarded information to use against you!—I'm only asking a simple question."

Molly is hurt, incensed. She knows Jonathan is offended; knows she should not pursue this subject. It is like leaning forward as she lights a candle, dreamily, watching as her long hair sweeps dangerously close to the flame.

"Well, I don't know the answer to your question," Jonathan says. "I'm sorry."

"You must know whether your brother went through the same training as you did—obviously," Molly says with an incredulous laugh. "I realize you're angry at him—you don't see him any longer—I can understand that, I'm not interrogating you about *that*—but you must at least know whether he was in school with you? At Harvard, wasn't it? Or was it somewhere in New York?''

"Why are you asking me this? Why now?" Jonathan asks.

"Now? I—I really don't know—''

"Why now? Tonight? This minute? When we've both had exhausting days—or at least I've had an exhausting day? Why now, why do you want to ruin everything?''

Molly thinks, dazed, as if suddenly slapped, that it is impossible to get through this man's defense. He matches one question with another, so deftly you would think he had planned his strategy beforehand. Yet he seems scarcely to know what he does.

She says, "Jonathan, I only asked a simple question.''

She knows she should stop but she persists; as if, daringly, she *must* lean forward to see how closely her hair can come before it bursts into flame. "I only asked a simple question, I don't see why you're so upset. I would have thought it an innocent question. But forget it, please—your brother is obviously a sore point with you and—''

Jonathan says angrily, " 'Sore point'!—what a thing to say. What vulgar, trivial language! 'Sore point'! Really! And what do *you* know about it?''

Molly presses her hands over her ears. "I'm sorry! Forget it, please!''

"You sound suddenly like the shallow-minded person you told me you were afraid of turning into, or being," Jonathan says. " 'Sore point'—your very use of language—it's so flippant, so vulgar—to allude to something profoundly serious about which you know nothing—''

Molly is going to stand her ground but, no, Molly had better retreat, she's staring at her lover and thinking, Why? why?—why is he so angry at *me?*—staring at this man with the blood-darkened face, the narrowed eyes, that look of contempt and fury and impotence, thinking, *I don't know him at all, I don't know him any more than I know the other.* But of course this is absurd: Jonathan McEwan is the man Molly loves and will marry. She begins to cry and touches him and will in a moment press herself into his arms knowing he'll relent, he'll forgive, he'll accept her acquiescence—"Please, Jonathan, I'm sorry," she says. "I'm truly sorry."

And I am, Molly thinks, sobered. I truly am.

What *had* begun the quarrel?—Molly would not care to remember but a few days later, casually, with an air of husbandly repentance, Jonathan says, "The other night you were saying you thought you'd been 'cured' of some problems . . . ? What do you mean, Molly? Do you mean you'd like to resume psychotherapy?"

"No, not at all," Molly says at once. She laughs faintly. "My God! *No.*"

But Jonathan regards her with an air of tenderness, gravity, compassion. As if he'd wronged her and must make amends. "When we terminated our professional relationship," he says, "I offered to refer you to another therapist. And, if you like, if you feel the need, I can still do that. If you're still unhappy, and evidently you are . . . or think you are."

"I'm not unhappy at all," Molly says. "I'm very happy."

"The other night you were saying . . ."

"I don't remember, Jonathan. Really."

Molly looks genuinely puzzled, squinting up at him.

"I'm not unhappy," she says. "That's absurd."

"*I* don't think there's anything in the slightest wrong with you," Jonathan says, relieved. "But that might be my prejudice, of course. Since I love you. Adore you."

Molly kisses him and says, "And I love you. Adore you."

"Even at our first interview, that day—you struck me, Molly, as a normal young woman, a mild casualty of the age, if anything, but stronger and more resilient and far more canny than most—going through some very natural emotional phases. The things you *said* about yourself had a neurotic ring, of course, yet the way you said them, *you* as you said them, seemed to belie their significance. Of course," he says, "that might be my prejudice."

Molly pokes Jonathan in the ribs. "You thought I was a silly little twat, did you!"

Jonathan says, "Molly!—what a thing to say. Of course not."

"What *did* you think?"

"That I adored you. It was love at first sight," Jonathan says. Winding his fist gently in Molly's long hair.

And so another time the subject has been deflected.

5 "I have never been able to decide whether life is serious or comic. Which is why I suppose I joke a lot. And the jokes aren't funny."

"Tell me a joke!"

"A—a joke? Now? I can't think of one."

"Invent one!"

"I—I don't think I can. I'm sorry—"

"Hurry! Now! As if your life depends upon it!"

"I can't. Please, I—"

"Tell me a joke."

"Why are you wearing so much clothing?"

"So much clothing—?"

"I count several layers. And different textures—weights."

"Because it's cold."

"It isn't cold."

"It *is*—for me."

"And why do you sit huddled like that?"

"I'm not huddled."

"Tense as a bow. Bent and ready to spring."

"I'm not."

"Hugging yourself."

"I'm *not.*"

"Is it to give me the idea of hugging you?"

"No. Certainly not."

"Why *certainly* not?"

"Why did you come back?"

"I don't know."

"Why did you come back when you were so angry?"
"I really don't know!"
"Is it because you want to be cured?"
"Yes, I suppose so. Of course."
"But of what do you want to be cured?"
"My—problems."
"Problems, or problem?"
"I suppose—problem. I suppose there is only one."
"And what do you suppose that is?"
"I—I don't know."
"You do know."
"I don't! I've come to you to find out."
"That isn't why you've come to me."
"It is."
"Don't you know why you've come to me?"
"Why I've come to you—? I—I've said: to be cured."
"But of what?"
"Don't do this to me!"
"What am I doing to you?"
"Squeezing my brain out of shape—"
"And does it hurt?"

"Do you know the ancient Chinese proverb: 'When one dog begins barking at a shadow, ten thousand make it into a reality'? And you understand it?"
"No. I mean yes."
"You're cured."

"Come here."
"I—I'd rather not."
"Come here and undress me."
"I can't do that."
"Since you want to, you must."
"I don't want to."
"Don't you?"
"I don't."
"Then why are you here?"
"I—I've told you."
"To be cured? But you are cured."

"No I'm not."

"Why do you look at me as you do?"

"How do I look at you?"

" 'He who desires but acts not, breeds pestilence.' "

"I—I don't desire you."

"Don't you?"

"I don't."

"Then why are you here, and why do you keep returning?"

"To learn—"

"Yes?"

"To learn a truth about—"

"Yes?"

"Myself, and others."

"Then come here."

6 "Unless twins work hard at separating their identities, they are always in danger of becoming psychic monsters."

Molly Marks reads (in secret: when she should be working, at the office, or, in the evening, when Jonathan thinks she is reading another kind of book entirely) about twins and the history of twins, twins as a sign of wonder and twins as a sign of horror, twins as taboo, twins as divine. In classical mythology Zeus rapes the mortal woman Leda in the form of a swan and from that union, out of the egg of that union, are born the twins Castor and Polydeuces—twins of perpetual combat. There are the Biblical twins Jacob and Esau, Pharez and Zarah. There were the famous "Siamese" twins physically joined at the torso—a monster of a kind, yet two fully individualized human beings. Primitive tribes of Australia and Africa traditionally murdered one or even both of a set of twins at birth, and sometimes the women who had given birth. Yet elsewhere, at other times, twins were considered emblems of fertility, and their mothers honored. In ancient Egypt . . . In ancient Scandinavia . . . In Tibet . . . Even today, among certain tribes of the Amazon. . . .

Molly Marks learns that there are approximately one hundred million twins in the world!—of which approximately one-third are identical. Molly learns that the distinction is always made between merely fraternal twins, born of two _____ zygotic), and identical twins, born of a single egg _____gotic). The former resemble each other, the latter, possessing identical sets of genes, *are*, in a purely biological sense, each other.

Sometimes, when one is hurt, the other feels pain; when one is ill, the other succumbs to the illness. They tend to die, accidents not barred, at around the same time.

Sometimes even into adulthood they feel that they are trapped in a single mind.

"Of course," Molly tells herself carefully, "—all this doesn't apply to individuals."

7 *"Don't* hurt me this time—I don't like it, really."

"Then why are you here? And why do you keep coming back?"

("I will answer my own question, dear Holly. You exemplify Thorndike's famous law of effect: we return repeatedly to the source of pleasure stimuli.")

"Don't you love me a little?—don't you *like* me? I think you do."

"What grounds do you have for thinking that?"

"Am I mistaken?"

"I will admit that I'm attracted to you. Obviously."

"Thank you!"

"And it delights me that you're so obviously attracted to *me*. Men find that as flattering as women do."

"I don't mean to flatter. It's genuine."

"And is it 'genuine' with your lover too?"

"My lover—is very different from you."

"Is he?"

"I would say so, yes."

"Would he be jealous of me?"

"My God, yes."

"Would he stop loving you, if he knew?"

"I—I don't know."

"What do you think?"

"I think—he would be very hurt; but he would forgive me."

"How could he forgive you if you continue to see me?"

"I'd break it off with you, if he knew."

"Then you love me less than you love him."

"Yes because I don't really know you. I only know—this."

"And do you think you know *him?*"

"I know him better than I know you."

"And is he a good man, as you've suggested? Good, kind, strong, reliable, steadfast—all the old tested virtues?"

"Oh yes."

"He isn't like me at all."

"In superficial ways, perhaps."

"What sorts of superficial ways?"

"Appearance—superficially."

"And which of us is more attractive?"

"I—I can't know."

"Can't or won't say?"

"Can't."

"But why is that?"

"When I'm with him I think of you; when I'm with you—I think of him."

"Oh no you don't."

"This caption under Nietzsche's photograph—is it from a letter? Is it a joke? 'Dear Herr Professor, When it comes to it I too would very much prefer a professorial chair in Basel to being God; but I did not dare to go as far in my private egoism as to refrain for its sake from the creation of the world.' What does it mean?"

"It means precisely what the words say."

"Was Nietzsche mad?"

"As Nietzsche, or as God?"

"I will admit I'm attracted to you. But there isn't much room in my life for you right now."

"I'm small—I don't take up much room." Says Molly Marks. Or is it Holly Hawkes—?

8 When Molly Marks first moved to Lindesfarne, Connecticut, she had a tortoiseshell cat named St. Ives—big, burly, lazy, cranky and sweet-natured by turns. She'd taken on St. Ives as a favor to a Provincetown friend who was spending a summer in Italy and when the friend returned and failed to pick up St. Ives Molly thought, annoyed, relieved, That's fate. She had not wanted to be tied down with the responsibility of a pet— Molly Marks didn't want to be tied down with much responsibility at all—but she'd grown fond of the creature and did not much mind his dramatic swings of mood which may have mimicked Molly's own.

The story of some lives, Molly thought, is mainly the story of a succession of pets—Christ save me from *that*.

Still, she and St. Ives got on. Sometimes Molly shouted at him, "You're my only friend, damn you—a *cat.*"

When men came to visit Molly—when men came, as they invariably did, to spend the night with Molly—St. Ives had a disconcerting habit of forcing the door of Molly's bedroom in the middle of the night and leaping onto her bed, mewing querulously. When Molly was alone he sometimes took an inscrutable feline revenge by keeping his distance, except of course when being fed. At other times he would throw himself against her like one of her less favored suitors demanding to be petted, scratched, fussed over, loved. He'd grown so heavy—not exactly fat: heavy—that Molly staggered beneath his weight when she tried to carry him. His baritone purr vibrated against her chest.

The first evening Jonathan McEwan came to Molly Marks's

apartment for dinner Molly noticed him staring at St. Ives with a look of extreme interest verging on dread. They were not yet lovers but they were of course intensely attracted to each other, at this time psychotherapist and "client"—the one rather guiltily, the other with an air of childlike passivity and expectation: let him, let him, dear God let this man love me not as I deserve to be loved but as I *want* to be loved! (So Molly Marks shamelessly prayed, and not always silently, a dozen times a day, those days.) Ever alert to a guest's discomfort, Molly was moved to ask if Jonathan was allergic to cats. "No," Jonathan said politely. "I mean—I don't know that I am."

"Some people don't like cats on principle, they have phobias about them," Molly suggested, but Jonathan, not yet very at ease with her, and certainly not at ease in St. Ives's presence, stiffened at the suggestion. "The clinical term is ailurophobia," he said, "—but that doesn't apply to me."

Molly asked Jonathan if he had any pet or pets of his own and he told her he sometimes kept turtles, usually not for long but until he felt the impulse to free them. He often found turtles injured on roads, or for sale at flea markets or bazaars—the poor creatures heaped atop one another, cruelly mistreated. Did she know, Jonathan asked Molly, that when young turtles' shells are painted for commercial reasons the shells are unable to grow in proportion to their bodies, with the result that, in time, the turtles' bodies are squeezed out of shape, and they die? Sometimes Jonathan bought up a vendor's entire stock of such turtles and took them home and tried to remove the paint on their shells as best he could. . . . He was speaking rather heatedly now and he broke off, embarrassed. "Sorry," he told Molly. "I get carried away on the subject."

Molly thought, What a good-hearted man!

Molly thought, This is the man to save *me*.

But Jonathan did not like St. Ives, no matter that he tried to, and laughed to show he was a good sport when, to Molly's extreme embarrassment, St. Ives forced open Molly's bedroom door and charged in at a particularly awkward moment. "He's jealous," Molly said apologetically. Jonathan said,

"No—*I'm* jealous." But that was the last night St. Ives asserted himself quite so dramatically. After that Molly gave St. Ives to a neighbor to keep on those nights Jonathan stayed with her, and when she and Jonathan leased their apartment together the young woman volunteered to keep St. Ives, of whom she'd grown fond. "He has a certain way about him," she said.

Molly, giving up St. Ives for Jonathan McEwan, considered she'd made the better of the deals.

When, in early December, James McEwan first brings Molly Marks to his apartment (the highest floor of the brownstone on East 83rd Street), she is astonished to see that he owns a tortoiseshell cat so very like St. Ives she thinks, for an unsettling moment, that it *is* St. Ives—sleek, well-fed, insolent, with identical markings about the face, and near-identical tawny eyes.

This can't be, Molly thinks. She is already in a nerved-up state, having come to James's apartment with him when she should be on her way back to Lindesfarne; and the sight of her old cat, curled on a sofa, blinking lazily at her, is nearly too much for her.

"Your cat—he reminds me of a cat I used to own," Molly tells James. "The resemblance is uncanny."

"That's Danton," James says. "He comes with the apartment, so to speak. No one really owns him."

James helps Molly take off her coat. As he explains, in his amused, slightly drawling manner, the circumstances behind his ownership of a cat—he, who isn't at all sentimental about animals, and only tolerates this one because it gives absolutely no sign of being dependent on him—Molly draws closer, under the pretext of wanting to stroke Danton's head, and sees to her considerable relief that it isn't, of course, St. Ives after all. The beautiful swirls of color in this animal's coat—black, brown, orange, tawny-blond, white—differ significantly from the swirls of color in St. Ives's coat. And Danton has fierce jet-black whiskers while St. Ives's were a milder shade of brown. Or so Molly remembers.

"The resemblance *is* uncanny," she says.

"But surely not important," James McEwan says, bored with the subject.

He slips his arms around Molly, his hands—quick, greedy, teasing—up inside Molly's silk blouse. He pinches her breasts—her hardened nipples. "That hurts," Molly protests. He kisses her neck; closes his arms so tightly around her rib cage she winces in pain. "That *hurts,*" Molly says. *"Please."* James says, his breath warmly damp against her ear, "Why else did you come here?"

Molly extricates herself from him and pushes away: legs like storks' legs—frail, blundering, unsteady. The apartment is flooded with stark winter sunlight but she can't seem to see. She's excited, aroused, apprehensive, incredulous—thinking, as she tucks her blouse in the waistband of her skirt, adjusts her pretty little sleeveless crocheted sweater, He won't rape me will he! He isn't a maniac is he!

"Why else did you come here, 'Holly'?" James McEwan asks, close behind her.

There is no trouble about Molly Marks taking each Thursday afternoon off from work: the partners are anxious to accommodate her, she's "such an asset." They sense she is overqualified for the work she's been doing and may in fact be restless, ready to move on. Nor is there trouble with Jonathan. If he is hurt that Molly resumed psychotherapy sessions with a therapist in Manhattan recommended to her by a woman friend, and not with one of his acquaintances, he gives no sign—he is too gentlemanly, too kind. The Manhattan therapist's name is Wexler—Dr. Agnes Wexler. "Agnes Wexler, yes," says Jonathan. "I've heard very good things about her. You couldn't be in better hands."

Molly thought, My heart is broken—lying to this man.

Molly thought, I *am* crazy, then—of course!

The drive from Lindesfarne, Connecticut, to East 83rd Street in Manhattan is approximately seventy miles each way—a bracing distance, Molly Marks thinks: just far enough. Her new car is a sporty little canary-yellow Honda hatchback she loves to drive and, no, she isn't the sort of woman who worries about going into the city alone.

She needed, she told Jonathan, to get out of Lindesfarne at least once a week, just needed more space, more air. And it made, she said, coming back home all the sweeter. "I feel the same way," Jonathan said, "—but I don't have to go so far away in order to come back."

When, in November, Molly saw James McEwan again in his office, she did not faint at the very sight of him though she did, to her embarrassment, feel a wave of dizziness so palpable she half thought the psychotherapist must feel it too. But she controlled herself. She spoke calmly, intelligently. She, Holly Hawkes.

She told Dr. McEwan that while she strongly disapproved of his professional method—his "bullyboy tactics"—she *did* believe nonetheless that he could help her. As no other psychotherapist could help her.

"Really?" said James McEwan, staring at her intently. "What a wonderfully extravagant thing to declare!"

His smile was Jonathan's smile—with a look of something wired and barbed about it. Not sweetness but mock-sweetness of course. Molly thought angrily, But I'm lying to you, you smug bastard. *I* know what I'm doing.

(I want to know what you did to Jonathan. And what you made him do.)

"I *had* to see you again," Molly whispered.

"Of course," said James McEwan.

It was a November afternoon, a twilit day rapidly descending to dusk. Prematurely cold—sharply cold—the air smelling like iron. Molly Marks—that is to say, Holly Hawkes—was shivering though she'd done herself up stylishly in layers of clothing, a long-sleeved silk blouse, a hand-crocheted little vest sweater, a cashmere wool jacket and a cashmere wool skirt that fell fashionably to mid-calf. She wore textured stockings, knee-high boots with a considerable heel. And the slope-brimmed hat Jonathan thought so charming, also cashmere, wonderfully soft to the touch. Her hair wasn't loose this time but braided and wound prettily around her head and her face fairly glared with a perfect porcelain sheen—she'd noted with satisfaction people glancing at her in the street. Actress? Model? *Who . . . ?*

If James McEwan was surprised to see her again in his office, or surprised at the transformation in her appearance, he gave no indication. When Molly had gone to her second session with Jonathan looking very different from the way she'd looked for the first he had, she thought, expressed *some* surprise—was it normal not to?

"You didn't think I'd come back, did you?" she said finally.

"My dear," said James McEwan, "I didn't think about you at all. Did you intend me to?"

Now *they* are lovers—in a manner of speaking.

Solely, Molly thinks, in a manner of speaking.

Holly Hawkes, James McEwan. "Lovers" on a once-a-week basis and, as James has made clear, ah so unflatteringly clear, it is *only* once-a-week and it is *only* for a finite period of time. "You know what 'no-fault' liability insurance is?" James says. Molly says, laughing, "Right!"

He does acknowledge she is a beautiful woman, a desirable woman—there is that, at least.

And he admires her style, as he calls it. Her flair for putting clothes together, making up her face, doing weird wild unexpected things with her hair. And her flair for love-making of a certain kind—though she has, still, a good deal to learn.

"But we won't rush it," James says affably. "That's been my mistake in the past—impatience."

The man's cynicism fascinates Molly. It is so unstudied, so matter-of-fact, it reminds her, in a way, of Jonathan McEwan's idealism: each man speaks with absolutely no hesitation, not the slightest nuance of ambiguity.

James tells her, as perhaps he tells all his clients, that, yes, he can "cure" her of one or another mental snarl but is it worth it? Is *she* worth it? (James McEwan doesn't come cheap, as he'd warned. Nor does he make any concession, give any discount, so to speak, since Holly Hawkes has become sexually available to him.) Man is the amoral animal, James says, finding reasons for what he (or she) intends to do anyway; nobody has the slightest notion of what he is doing, or why, but—"The 'neurotic' is one who insists upon knowing."

"That, at least, places us in a slightly higher category?" Molly says ironically.

"Yes, I grant you that," James says. "But only *slightly* higher."

He laughs happily and adds, "A man in my position has so many advantages!—*this,* of course." (Meaning Molly, lying coiled in his arms.) "But also the fact that, in order to keep on this side of madness, you must frequent those more demented than yourself."

How I loathe you, Molly Marks thinks.

"How nastily brilliant you are," Molly Marks says, forcing herself to laugh.

"It sounds as if your lover, whoever he is, the 'man in your life,' is a man very different from me," James says, amused.

"Yes," says Molly. "He is."

"And you're proud of him?—of 'having' him, that is."

"I suppose I am," Molly says.

"And you think it will last?"

"I—I think it will last."

"I suppose you plan to have a baby—'start a family' one day soon?"

"I—"

"Poor girl! How frightened you are!"

But James is only amused; only teasing. He might pity her but his pity doesn't stand in the way of his mockery. He plays at comforting her as one might comfort a child, using his hands and mouth; then, with no warning, he begins tickling her, her armpits, her belly, between her legs, his fingers hard and swift, giving pain. Molly struggles, laughing and breathless, protesting, "Please don't," and "Don't—*really,*" and "God damn you, you bastard—"

Until finally Molly is aroused herself, breathless and panting and eager for sexual pleasure that is stark and piercing—killing. They make love—in a manner of speaking—clutching and pummeling at each other's flesh, love cries in the air like shrieking birds. James, inside her, is quick and arrhythmic as if he wants to elude her rhythm, the pulse and beat of her own sensation; he's a heavy man, and has no mercy for her as Jonathan does—dear Jonathan, with whom Molly is so slow and ardent, so awash in tears of sentiment. The peaks and shallows of James's pleasure are erratic—he can't be predicted. Sometimes he finishes within seconds, at other times he will make love to Molly roughly, jocularly, patiently, for a very long time—hunched over her smiling and teasing, "Shut your eyes, hussy!" and "Show some modesty, girl!" To Jonathan lovemaking is a sacred ritual, to James it is an engaging physical act. He drips, and seems to like dripping, oily globules of sweat on Molly; he laughs at her straining face, her drowning eyes and anguished O of a mouth. Beneath his healthy bulk the bed—an enormous king-sized bed—rocks like a comically storm-tossed boat.

"Don't, dear, be embarrassed. Please."

James lies with his hands behind his head, kinky glistening hairs sprouting from his armpits. His color is blood-warmed, rich; there are tucks and creases in his skin, bracketing his mouth, so very like Jonathan's that Molly would not know which man it is except for James's posture, and his dreamy arrogant manner . . . a certain blood-suffused thickness to his lips. And it is daylight. Jonathan rarely makes love to Molly by day. Nor does he contemplate her like this, as if she were an object of delectation.

Sometimes, with Jonathan, Molly feels invisible—she's so cherished. With James she knows that she is irremediably visible. And he likes to look.

"Don't be embarrassed. You were quite charming."

"I've never done anything like that before." Molly is rather breathless; on the edge of being frightened. She supposes the remark is much-heard, by this man, whether it happens to be true or not.

"Yes, love, but you've fantasized it, like all women. Which comes to the same thing."

* * *

"You do seem," James McEwan says, his tone edged with impatience, "unusually taken with that cat."

"Oh no—not really."

"You watch him rather oddly. And if I didn't suppose it was entirely my imagination, I'd say he watches you rather oddly in turn."

Molly laughs. "Well—I did have a cat, once, that resembled him. To a degree."

"And that cat is associated with a happier, easier time in your life?—since, darling, you gaze at him so wistfully."

"Happier, no. Easier, yes."

"How you flatter! It's one of the things you're good at," James says. "This cat. Did you wrong him?"

"Wrong him? Of course not. I was very fond of him, really."

"Which doesn't preclude your wronging him, does it?"

Molly laughs again, uneasily.

"You'll note that I speak of your former pet as 'him'," says James, "knowing in fact it was a male. Because all tortoiseshell cats are male."

"Really?"

"And all tortoiseshell cats are twins."

"Twins?"

"You don't know about their genetic eccentricity?"

"Genetic eccentricity?"

"You sound like a parrot, dear, or an echo. Yes, tortoiseshells are unique creatures in that each is twins."

"I see," Molly says slowly. "Twins."

"But did you hear me, love? I said each *is* twins."

James is smiling dreamily into space; leaning back against the oversized pillows in a posture of utter relaxation, his hands clasped behind his head. Molly regards him slantwise as if fearing to look him in the face. His skin, close up, always seems blinding, as if lit from within.

(Jonathan has lost his summer tan months ago but James still has his; he must use a sunlamp. He looks, Molly thinks resentfully, so damned *healthy* after they've made love.)

"Each is twins? What do you mean? Out of the same litter?"

Molly's remark is both stupid and senseless but she doesn't know what else to say, the subject excites her so.

James repeats as if speaking to a young child or a mentally defective person: *"Tortoiseshells are unique creatures in that each is twins."*

"I don't understand," Molly says nervously.

"They're freaks of nature," says James. "Each contains double genes. When the mother cat's egg is fertilized in the womb twin fetuses form but for some reason—ah, what pranks Nature plays!—the fetuses merge into a single organism within a few weeks: a single cat. But this cat will have the genetic material of both original twins."

"In one cat?" Molly asks, horrified.

"Fascinating, isn't it?"

"I don't believe it—*in one cat?*"

"The dominant twin, it might be called."

James smiles at her. She would know that smile, Molly thinks, on any face.

PART
TWO

9 Molly Marks studies Jonathan McEwan a dozen times a day without his knowing. If you really loved me, she thinks, you would tell me your secret. And I would never see *him* again.

For she must know the twins' secret. These many weeks—months!—she thinks of *it*, and of *him*, and of *him*.

On the busy spinning surface of Molly Marks's life—her work for the three-man public relations outfit as a glorified Girl Friday (albeit well-paid, there's that compensation); the informal network of friends, acquaintances, professional associates she has hooked into by way of Jonathan McEwan (Molly is eager to repay Jonathan's friends' hospitality as a way of establishing her household with him and as a way— of course—of not thinking of James); burning off nervous energy at the local Nautilus fitness center ("Please don't get *too* fit, darling—no one likes muscles in pretty women!" James has said)—the only place, Molly thinks wryly, where loneliness *works*. She means to keep up her old scattered friendships—with women mainly—women are all that's left of entire years, seasons in her life—just as she means to keep up her "relationship" with her family but there isn't time. Never time!—happy thought. At least I know I'm alive, Molly tells herself.

Weekdays are fast, crowded, not always coherent: sometimes she and Jonathan scarcely see each other except at breakfast (if Molly is up and sociable) and in the evenings (if Jonathan isn't pressed for emergency work). Weekends they treasure, weekends are all they have. Seeing friends,

going out to films, concerts, plays. They drive along the coast
with no destination, holding hands. Sometimes they get as
far as Cape Cod. (The McEwan family owns a summer house
in Narragansett, Rhode Island, Jonathan says—but seems in
no hurry to take Molly there.) They discover new restaurants,
prepare experimental Chinese meals together in their modern, compact kitchen. They are a perfectly matched couple,
as observers note. So American, and so *contemporary*.

It's true, Molly is a little jealous of Jonathan's work. It
means something to him her own work doesn't mean to her.
She knows that his female clients, and very likely some of
his male clients, focus their neurotic (erotic?) energies on
him. "Transference," Molly tells him, "—that old black
magic!" She complains of his long hours as a psychotherapist—particularly at the Stamford clinic for which he isn't
paid. And Jonathan is always giving up one of their precious
weekends to deliver a paper at a psychology conference, or
to referee applications for foundation grants, or to write book
reviews for professional journals that pay contributors in off-
prints. Molly never nags—she isn't after all a wife—but she
knows that certain of Jonathan's associates take advantage of
him because he is so good-hearted, so generous, so kind. A
soft touch. Molly says, incensed, "You shouldn't let yourself
be pushed around like that, Jonathan!" Or Molly says: "Don't
you see how these people are manipulating you, Jonathan!"
She thinks he should cut back on some of his pro bono work,
she thinks he should turn over the worst of his clients' unpaid
bills to a collection agency. When Jonathan tells her his work
is none of her concern and she has no reason to get upset
about it, or about him, when, in fact, he tells her *he* is quite
satisfied with his professional life, Molly stalks off thinking
If the fool persists in his folly he grows more foolish still. It
is one of James McEwan's remarks, but not the most cynical.

"Maybe if you felt better about your own work," Jonathan
says shrewdly, "you wouldn't object to mine."

"That's a cruel thing to say. That's not worthy of you,"
Molly says, hurt.

"Maybe if you didn't object to my seeing Dr. Wexler,"
Molly says, "you wouldn't be so sarcastic with me."

"Sarcastic with you? Molly, when? —And I don't object to your seeing Dr. Wexler, haven't I made that clear?"

"Yes. No. I don't know," Molly says, suddenly furious.

(Does Jonathan object? Surely he *is* jealous? Molly thinks, He wouldn't be human if he wasn't jealous but, Christ, is he human!—the corners of her pretty mouth downturned like a gargoyle's.

Of course Jonathan, sweet gentlemanly Jonathan, professional integrity to his fingertips, would never bring himself to ask Molly about the specific nature of her Thursday afternoon appointments in New York City. Only in the most general, conversational of ways: "Are you learning something about yourself?"—smiling like a moderator on one of the nicer television talk shows. And Molly replies, deadpan, "Yes, I'm afraid so.")

It is December, eighteen days to Christmas. A cold still moonlit night. Molly Marks, splendidly dressed in a white silk-and-wool pants suit, glossy hair spilling past her shoulders, is drinking a little more than usual but holding her own, and better, at the convivial gathering in New Haven to which Jonathan McEwan has brought her—the most attractive woman at the party (as she is the youngest) but not, she guesses, the most spectacular. There are women professors from Yale here, there are women lawyers, a highly regarded woman psychologist who has recently published a book on Freud and feminism which Jonathan McEwan praised in print in the *Journal of Interpersonal Psychology,* for which he is an advisory editor. Molly Marks avoids these women knowing they will ask her what she does and she might say something flippant and embarrassing and outrageous (and defensive: like "Fuck") and Jonathan will be hurt, and Jonathan will love her a little less.

Molly watches Jonathan covertly and thinks, How would he look in *his* eyes? She was with James hardly twenty-four hours ago and is feeling, still, rather unreal.

Yes that's the feeling, rather: unreal.

Molly sips white wine and Molly hears herself being funny,

witty, gay it might be said or is it giddy, she isn't going to
think of yesterday's degrading session in James McEwan's
office (on the leather couch: a place, she guesses, of num-
berless quick connections over the years) and she isn't going
to think of the fact that James will be out of the city for three
weeks (in Barbados, staying at the palatial home of a "former
client") and she isn't going to think of James's casual revelation, when they kissed goodbye, that he knows about her
subterfuge—has known all along.

"Why do you persist, darling, in 'Holly Hawkes'?"

"What do you mean?—that's my name."

"When we first saw each other, on 57th Street I think it
was, last spring, you identified yourself as 'Molly.' Didn't
you?"

Molly stared speechless at him.

"—and you called me Jonathan, didn't you?" James said,
smiling. "An understandable mistake since we *are* identical
twins."

No Molly isn't going to think about it . . . Molly is going
to get drunk. After all, the Christmas season is rapidly approaching, and beyond it New Year's Eve and stark white
snowy blank New Year's Day. She has decided she will never
see James McEwan again. He timed his *coup* so it happened
just before leaving for Barbados so there is a natural break,
she has already told Jonathan that Dr. Wexler is going away
for three weeks. ("That doesn't seem very professional—she
should have taken her vacation in August," Jonathan said
mildly.) Oh never again!—such shame, humiliation, grovel-
ing for the basest sort of pleasure, like a baby screaming for
mother's milk. (Is semen a kind of milk?—Molly wonders if
the more poetic-speculative of psychologists have written on
the subject.)

Never, please God, again.

No more Holly Hawkes, in any case. It was like being
stripped rudely naked—her childish little imposture exposed.
And, being the man he is, supremely arrogant, indifferent,
uninterested in others' motives, James McEwan had not even
troubled to ask Molly why she'd done it; why it seems to
have meant so desperately much to her.

But Molly is enjoying the party, Molly always does enjoy parties. Set her in the midst of a gathering like this, drink in hand, and she's an animated windup doll, eyes shining, cheeks lightly flushed with excitement. When she has had too much to drink she is likely to say outrageous things but in the din no one will hear, or remember.

Molly notes with her old gloating satisfaction that a number of men at the party are distinctly interested in her. A few have jockeyed to be introduced to her, no doubt sniffing hurt, depravity, promise.

"Tell me about Jonathan," she commands one of them, identified as someone who has known Jonathan for a long time, "—he's very reticent about his background. His family. He has a brother, doesn't he? A twin?"

"I think so, yes," the man says evasively.

"Haven't you ever met him?—the twin?"

"I'm afraid not."

"But didn't they go to college together?"

"Did they? I don't know."

"Or to prep school—"

"That's back before my time in Jonathan's life."

The man is flattered by Molly's interest but not about to be seduced by her; not with Jonathan McEwan close by glancing now and then in their direction. Molly, however, leans forward coquettishly, you might say brashly, under cover of being charmingly drunk. "But why is there so much animosity between Jonathan and his brother, do you know?"

"*Is* there?" says the man carefully. "I'd never heard that."

"The brother is a psychotherapist too—I think his practice is in New York."

"Really."

"I think he did something cruel to Jonathan and Jonathan has never forgiven him—"

"Really."

"And Jonathan is still upset about it after all these years—"

"*Really.*"

Later that evening Molly pursues another professional colleague of Jonathan's, a therapist who practices in New Haven and who was a classmate, an exact contemporary, of Jonathan's, at one of the institutes at which Jonathan trained. She asks him if he knows Jonathan's brother and he says do you mean Jonathan's twin brother and Molly says yes and he says he doesn't know the man but he did meet him once, ten years ago or more, in Jonathan's company—the first and only time they met.

"Then he wasn't a classmate of yours too?" Molly says, disappointed.

"No, I think he went into training a few years after Jonathan. He was doing something else at the time—I don't remember what." The man smiles quizzically at Molly. "I'm afraid I don't even remember his name—something like Joel, Joseph—"

"James."

"—and I don't know anything about him now. If he's a practicing therapist he keeps a low profile—doesn't publish much, or at all; doesn't seem to be interested in the profession the way Jonathan is. But Jonathan, of course, is rather special."

"But you don't know anything more about James?"

"Not really. Why do you ask?"

"I'm just curious. Jonathan is so reticent about his family. . . ."

"I do remember that Jonathan's brother talked more than he did. He was a little more forceful, though not much. They looked remarkably alike even for identical twins—it was uncanny. Of course they dressed differently, wore their hair differently, you could see they were making an effort to behave, and to think, differently," he says, shaking his head as if amused, "but the mannerisms were there—little things like their voice intonations, the way they walked, held their heads, smiled—invisible to the brothers but perfectly visible to anyone else."

He laughs. Molly hates him. "It must be hell being twins," he says, "I never thought of it until now."

"I wouldn't know," Molly says politely, easing away.

It occurs to Molly (in her host's bathroom as she washes her hands and observes herself critically yet with some small satisfaction in the mirror: that smudged sleepy-seductive look of her eyes quite suits her) that the questions she has been asking about Jonathan McEwan are a mistake. For one thing, they will cause people to talk about her—and Jonathan; for another, they might get back to Jonathan one day.

Christ, Molly, you must be drunk.

Christ, Molly, must you risk *everything*.

It is Jonathan's privilege after all to refuse to talk about his brother just as it is Molly's privilege (not yet claimed since Jonathan hasn't pressed her) to refuse to talk about certain shadowy areas of her own life . . . not criminal or even particularly shameful episodes, but matters of which she isn't proud.

And she told him, perhaps she'd promised him, that she respected his privacy.

Except: *why* won't he tell her?

Except: can it be that Jonathan himself did something terrible about which he can't speak?

Molly regards herself in the mirror severely. She's drunk but not that drunk.

Jonathan reaches over to squeeze Molly's gloved hand and says, "You seemed to be enjoying yourself tonight, Molly— I'm so glad."

Molly says, "You mean I was drunk and shrill and embarrassed you in front of your friends."

Jonathan glances at her startled and Molly says quickly, "Only a joke, Jonathan. Only a joke."

After a strained pause she adds, "Your friends are very nice. I like them. I wish they liked me."

"Why do you say that, Molly? Of course they like you."

"They don't know me."

"That's a textbook classic. What does it mean?"

"You tell me what it means. You have all the answers."

Molly draws her hand out of Jonathan's. Her vision is filming over—or is there a gauzy texture to the moonlight? She thinks of James squeezing her hand hard, a little too hard. And the imprint of his fingers on her arm. And the scattering of bruises on her thighs which Jonathan would never notice, lacking all suspicion.

"I think you're right," Molly says, relenting, after another strained silence. "About my job. My succession of jobs. They aren't worthy of me—I need to be helping people, involved in a community, as you are. As it is all I do is make money—"

Jonathan laughs. "I wouldn't disparage that, Molly!"

"—and spend it. On useless things, mainly. Vanities."

(The little PR group for which Molly works has made tremendous headway, as it's called, in just the past six months. New clients, new accounts, telephones always ringing, a U.S. congressman with strong financial backing who wants his image "updated," a chemical solvent company that wants its image "upscaled"—after having lost a widely publicized lawsuit brought against it by the State Environment Commission.)

"Why are you so self-critical? Is Dr. Wexler behind this?"

"Jonathan," Molly says, almost pleading, "I'm not self-critical enough and you know it."

"I love you. I don't know anything."

"I don't want to be patronized."

"If it's patronizing to love you I can't help that can I?"

Molly wants suddenly to get out of the car. She can't breathe, she thinks, in this car.

Jonathan says cautiously, looking over at her, "Molly—what *is* it? You seem to have changed so much in the past few months."

"I don't know. You know."

"You mean about starting a family?"

Molly shrugs.

"I thought we'd talked it through. But if you— If you still feel strongly—" Jonathan's voice trails off. He is baffled, embarrassed. Perhaps Molly Marks frightens him? He is not the kind of man, despite his professional training, who talks readily, or even willingly, of intimate matters.

"I don't understand you," he says finally.

A flame licks over Molly's brain. She hears herself saying angrily, "Let me out. Stop the car."

"What?"

"Stop the car. Please."

Molly is turning the door handle, threatening to open the door, she'll fall out and kill herself at seventy miles an hour—Jonathan, astonished, pleads with her to calm down for Christ's sake, calm down they'll be home in ten minutes—Molly cries hoarsely, "Let me out *now!*"—so he has no choice but to brake the car to an emergency stop. And Molly Marks jumps out and runs stumbling in the icy gravel at the side of the road, white kidskin boots, tears blurring her mascara, a Crazy Jane performance of a kind she's never tried before, while Jonathan, astonished, calls after her. She hears James's voice, mocking. She sees James, seeing her, mocking. If she could only run, run—run until she collapsed into insensibility—

It is at least four miles to Lindesfarne and Molly Marks intends to cover the distance on foot, no matter that it is past two in the morning and she's exhausted—sobbing with frustration. The night air is damned cold but bracing. It's what she needs she thinks to clear her head but she's already out of breath trying to run in her Bloomingdale's high-heeled boots, a scrim of tears freezing on her cheeks, hair loose and blowing and as James McEwan has said she's so *extravagant.* And to what purpose?

She intends to make her own way home but Jonathan follows along behind her of course, at a discreet distance, to shield her from the glaring headlights of other cars and the unwelcome scrutiny of strangers. His own headlights are dimmed out of gallantry—that's what Jonathan McEwan is like.

Molly calls out, "Go away! Leave me alone! I want to be alone!"

But Jonathan only eases back another few yards, keeping Molly well in sight as she runs staggering and slipping in the icy gravel. Oh Christ thinks Molly, furious, he's respectful enough not even to shout at me to stop behaving like an idiot and climb back in the car. . . .

And afterward he won't accuse her of being a hysterical woman. No matter what, secretly, he thinks.

* * *

"I love you so, Jonathan—I don't deserve your love," Molly says quietly.

"Molly, don't be silly," says Jonathan, delighted. "Don't, please, say such extravagant things!"

10 Molly Marks has a recurring dream which, most mornings, she does her best to forget. But when it wakes her in the middle of the night she lies helpless thinking about it, seeing again its single stark image—a featureless face: egg-smooth, eyeless, mere indentations in the flesh where eyes should have been; and tiny pinched nostrils but no nose; a hairline crack to denote the mouth. It's a nightmare image yet she isn't terrified by it, she feels, rather, an *interest* in it that is almost clinical.

The face is a mask of skin, utterly blind, yet it is, she knows, a living face: it "belongs" to someone.

A living being, a person, a woman no doubt.

My twin? Molly wonders.

She doesn't tell Jonathan about it, why should she. If she wakes him in the night, stirring and thrashing in her sleep, she tells him sleepily it's nothing, only a dream, she's forgotten it already and will he hold her, comfort her for a few minutes?—of course he will.

11

"Did you miss me a little?"

"Of course, a little—can't you tell?"

Says James McEwan, "Nobody wants to hear about death unless it can be made amusing," and Molly, who is about to tell him of her mother's death, and her own various reactions to it, is cut short.

She laughs, shocked.

"You're absolutely right," she says.

"Why didn't you say anything to me earlier, if you knew who I was?—I mean, who I wasn't."

"Why should I? It seemed no real business of mine."

"No real business of yours!"

"Don't look so surprised. You aren't the first person to start psychotherapy under a pseudonym. 'Holly, Molly'—what's the difference?"

"But you knew I was with Jonathan."

"I didn't *know,* I *surmised.*"

"But weren't you curious?"

"Curious? Why?"

"I—I would just think, you know, you would be. Considering the circumstances—"

"Perhaps there are more intriguing circumstances, love, in my life."

One dark snowy January afternoon the telephone rings and James McEwan picks up the receiver as if Molly Marks isn't there, doesn't perhaps exist. They are upstairs in the brownstone, in his apartment, to be precise in his bed. But James is more interested in the telephone conversation (which will last a heartbreaking twenty minutes—animated, amused, punctuated with exclamatory asides and bursts of zestful laughter and the murmurous refrain *husband . . . your husband*) than in Molly Marks: that's clear.

So Molly eases discreetly out of bed and slips on one of James's silk kimonos and leaves the bedroom, closing the door behind her. Thou art strong but I am meek, Molly thinks, her fist-sized heart beating in rage.

Though, as she tells herself, these are the terms of the contract, after all. It doesn't matter what the arrogant son of a bitch does; *she* is a free agent.

As both McEwans have told her at one time or another.

Barefoot, covered in a fine fragrant film of cooling sweat, Molly wanders out into the enormous living room . . . and there is St. Ives, that is, Danton, lying sprawled on a windowsill, watching her. Waiting for her. Luminous green cat-gaze like something in a surrealist painting.

The handsome brownstone on East 83rd Street is owned free and clear by James McEwan, who lives on the top floor and practices psychotherapy on the ground floor and leases out two floors to tenants. "How beautiful!" Molly Marks exclaimed, stepping for the first time into the top floor apartment, faced with the dazzling white expanse of a living room that seemed as large as the entire apartment she and Jonathan rented. "How *nice.*" If envious Molly is so for herself alone, and not for Jonathan.

James McEwan's apartment looks, over all, like a showcase of rooms, a decorator's display in which no one lives. (With the notable exception of the master bedroom, much-used.) The living room is white on white—white walls, sumptuous white deep-piled carpet, even a white-lacquered grand piano. There is a curved sofa, contemporary-Empire, long as a small freight train thinks Molly, decked out with eight enormous pillows: subtly varying shades of white, oyster, oatmeal, beige. And here and there in the room vivid patches of color jarring as inappropriate puns: a love seat covered in black-gold-pink floral fabric, a Pop-Art-red plastic chair, a wet-glistening salmon-red marble coffee table. Stylish and vulgar and assured, like James McEwan himself.

Molly strokes Danton's hard head, scratches him vigorously behind the ears and under the chin as St. Ives used to demand. The cat's husky baritone rumble gives solace but within minutes, as always, Danton grows restless and turns away.

"Damn," Molly whispers, hurt.

Alone and unobserved she prowls the living room, this stark stylish soulless room, in search of information, evidence. James McEwan is hardly the sort of man to display family photographs yet there are, placed here and there on his bookshelves, as if strategically, small framed photographs of him (looking so like Jonathan, Molly's heart stops!) posed with tennis racket, golf club, in swimming trunks, on the sloping deck of a yacht in full sail, smiling suntanned sunglassed James rarely photographed alone but in the company of others whom Molly guesses are client-friends, male and female. Some of the women are very good-looking indeed, standing close beside James McEwan and smiling hard into the camera, often with an arm, braceleted, linked snug through his. Molly wonders which of the women is the one with the winter home in Barbados. Or is there more than one.

Why feel sick with jealousy, envy, hurt, anger—whatever; it's hopeless in any case. James isn't Jonathan. James doesn't love her. James doesn't *love*. He has quoted Nietzsche to Molly in the most intimate of moments, and postures: " 'Ultimately one loves one's desire, not the desired object.' " He has laughed at her silly tears and has held a mirror against her face inviting her to laugh too.

James's clients are for the most part wealthy neurotics. They have nothing seriously wrong with them—if they did, he says, he wouldn't touch them with a ten-foot pole—so they are easily helped; and immensely grateful for help. And generous in their gratitude. And loyal as friends, benefactors, financial advisors, long after Dr. McEwan has pronounced them "cured."

These people require him in their lives, James says; they require him *for* their lives. Some of them have been taking

therapy with him three days a week for as long as he has
been practicing in New York—which is to say, eight years.
They have all improved, to a degree: they have gotten older
and therefore inevitably wiser. James McEwan is their soul-
doctor but he is also their friend, in a sense their only friend.
("As I am probably your only friend, dear Molly.") But
where friendship always precludes truth, as, certainly, love
precludes truth, in James McEwan's case where he befriends
and where he loves *he will not lie*—"Which sets me apart
from all but a very small fraction of humanity."

"You don't lie? You're incapable of lying?" Molly asks
skeptically.

"Did I say incapable? Unbribable."

Molly inspects James's shelves and sees to her surprise that
many of them duplicate Jonathan's shelves . . . book after
book after book. The book spines, the dust jackets, are un-
cannily familiar to her, even the height of certain oversized
books relative to books squeezed in beside them. "I don't
want to see this," Molly thinks. "I don't want to know this."
She takes down a book at random, a textbook on physiolog-
ical psychology, leafs through the pages and sees notations
in pencil and blue ballpoint pen that might be Jonathan's
notations; the handwriting is precisely the same. (Though
James *is* right-handed—Molly has seen him write—and Jonathan is left-handed. And it is beginning to strike Molly as
odd, even clumsy and unnatural—Jonathan's use of his left
hand.)

It is not surprising that James owns highly sophisticated
and surely very expensive stereophonic high-fidelity equip-
ment, one recessed wall given over to it, with shelves of
recorded music reaching nearly to the ceiling. Molly examines the neatly arranged rows of record albums and sees,
again, to her discomfort, that many of the titles duplicate
Jonathan's. (Though James has many more records than Jonathan, and has a collection of cassettes and disks as well.
And he has a full shelf of electronic music, which Jonathan
deplores as anti-music.) But here is the exact recording of
Debussy's early songs that Jonathan owns, and here is an
album of Tommasini that Jonathan owns, here the identical

Max Reger ("Twelve Pieces for Organ"), the identical Albinoni, Stravinsky, Ravel, Brahms, Benjamin Britten. Gould's Bach, Schnabel's Beethoven, Rachmaninoff's Rachmaninoff, identical recordings of Gregorian chant, medieval masses, Renaissance songs. Molly is amused, or is she alarmed, to see, here and there, albums identical to ones she herself bought for Jonathan: the most recent being a collection of Irish songs in a bright marbled-green cover.

Now that *is* nothing but coincidence isn't it. .

Molly pokes about the room, Molly opens drawers, Molly stands for a long time admiring a shelf of elegant jade figurines affixed to a mirrored section of the wall. Jonathan doesn't own a single jade figurine, to Molly's knowledge; but she guesses a gift of one would please him. How beautiful, Molly, he would say, smiling at her. He would never know what inspired her.

"Ah. Love. What *are* you doing?"

Molly cries out in fright as James comes up silently behind her. She had not seen his reflection in the mirror until he was upon her, closing his arms around her and lifting her as one might lift a naughty child, to chide and to scare. His fingers close over her breasts, his groin pumps against her buttocks in play but it's a rough startling play and Molly doesn't like it.

"—nosing about in my things? And what, dear Molly, have you found?"

Afterward she thinks that, the worst of it was, she'd glanced up and seen Jonathan in the mirror. Jonathan smiling and the smile shifting, twisting, veering into James's smile: "What *are* you doing?"

(Yes their hair whorls in opposite directions but it *is* the same hair, precisely—texture, thickness, springiness, degree of silvery-gray streaks and shadings. Their bodily hair is identical too though—unless Molly imagines it, which might very well be the case—James's pubic hair is more profuse, scratchier. Their genitals are identical if not their sexual appetites and proclivities and their lean pale buttocks are identical and their knobby knees, long toes, discolored toenails. If their teeth tend to decay on opposite sides of their mouths Molly can't know but, in all, their teeth look very much alike. Each has a slightly jagged left incisor that gives him, to Molly's romantic eye, a rakish razorish air, like Mack the Knife.

The brothers share a considerable number of tastes, mannerisms, living habits, but Molly doesn't know how to gauge the significance of these similarities. Coincidence? genetic determinism? extrasensory perception of which neither man is aware? When Jonathan smokes he holds his cigarette in his right hand, and, exhaling smoke, has a habit of screwing up the right half of his face; James holds his cigarette in his left hand, and, exhaling a luxurious cloud of smoke, screws up the left side of his face. Jonathan appears to smoke only when he is unhappy while James, who is never, evidently, unhappy, smokes when he pleases. James smokes the brand of cigarettes Jonathan smoked when Molly first knew him; now Jonathan is trying other brands, less potent, and less satisfying, in an effort to stop smoking entirely.

Both brothers use the same brand of razor blades, deodorant, aspirin, toothpaste . . . though James squeezes the toothpaste tube anywhere he wishes while Jonathan squeezes it from the end and neatly rolls it—of course. When, once, Molly stealthily opened the top drawer of James's bedroom bureau she found herself staring down into Jonathan's drawer—socks balled together in precisely the same way, the same scattering of tie clips, cuff links, a black plastic shoehorn. James owns a half-dozen wristwatches (of which all but two are gifts from clients) but one of them is Jonathan's watch. James's clothes are more expensive and more stylish than Jonathan's of course, and he has many more of them, but here and there in James's wardrobe is a sports coat, a shirt, a necktie, even a jaunty russet-red fedora, also owned by Jonathan. Like most conservative-minded men Jonathan McEwan makes startling purchases now and then, apparently on blind impulse—and these are likely to be items already owned by James.

How humiliated Jonathan would be, if he knew. And how amused, James, if *he* knew.

James's taste in food and drink is far more eclectic than Jonathan's but their eating habits, Molly has discovered, are alarmingly similar . . . so much so that, many an evening in Lindesfarne, she glances across the table at Jonathan and sees his brother in his place: a sight that quite unnerves her. Then Jonathan's gaze meets hers, and he smiles, and, yes, of course, it *is* . . . Jonathan. Eating, both men display considerable appetite, appropriate to their size; they have an inclination to hunch over their plates, heads just perceptibly lowered; their massive jaws tear, bite, chew, grind—Molly is reminded of big cats, feeding.

James walks Molly to the parking garage off Lexington where she has left her car. He has to go in that direction anyway, he says, might as well walk with her, he's tall robust bareheaded in the glow of streetlights at dusk and the lightly falling snow that melts on his skin, his perpetually heated skin. Molly, shorter than he by a head, slips her arm through his. Snug. She laughs when, at an icy curb, he lifts her and swings her over, to the startled delight of passersby. "We make an attractive couple," James admits, catching sight of their reflections in car windows as they pass, in the smooth-coppery surface of the doors, twin, of a pretentious Italian restaurant at the corner of 85th and Lexington. "But of course it's only genetic."

12 And a few days later in Lindesfarne when Molly and Jonathan are leaving a locally popular health food store where they buy the special chewy grainy whole wheat bread Jonathan loves they encounter a young woman named Jenny who runs a secretarial service in the office building in which Molly's public relations business rents space and the young woman who is a friend of Molly's though not a social friend exactly (meaning Molly will never invite Jenny to dinner though she might very well invite her, indeed intends to invite her, to a large heterogenous cocktail party) smiles at them and says, "I saw you two in New York last week—and you didn't see me waving."

Jenny is Molly's age, pretty, and freckled, and divorced, and perpetually cheerful as if on principle: sometimes a little too perky for Molly's wavering taste; and too damned familiar. Jonathan scarcely knows her so it falls to Molly to say, quickly, smiling hard to show that, no, she isn't upset, isn't even annoyed, she's simply correcting a very minor mistake, "Last week? No—I don't think so—we weren't in New York last week."

Jenny plants herself squarely in front of them, looking from one to the other. "But I *saw* you, Molly. I'm sure I did. You and Jonathan both."

"No, really," Molly says, pulling discreetly at Jonathan's arm, "—you must have seen someone else."

"But it looked just *like* you—the two of you. I could swear."

"We haven't been to New York together in months," Molly

87

says. She's terrified of course but seems to be on automatic pilot: playing out the scene as naturally as if her lines were being fed to her by a prompter just offstage. "I go in sometimes, alone—once in a while. But that's all."

"I could *swear,*" Jenny says, quizzical, smiling, glancing up at Jonathan as if hoping for his corroboration, "—but of course I could be mistaken, it was across a street, there were a lot of people around—"

"We might have doubles, too," Molly says, easing Jonathan away, "—I'm always being mistaken for someone else."

At the car Jonathan says, "Is that so, Molly? I didn't know that."

Molly is trembling now, her hands visibly shaking, but she looks up at Jonathan calmly enough and says, "What? What didn't you know?"

"That you're often mistaken for someone else."

"Well," says Molly, swallowing hard, deciding to stay with the lie, "—it's so."

The next day Molly meets Jenny and feels a wash of guilt but smiles and says hello, friendly as ever, and Jenny's friendly too, warm and smiling as ever. Jenny says apologetically, "I guess I was mistaken the other day?" and Molly says carefully, "Well—it's nothing, really." Jenny says, "It looked so much like you and Jonathan, coming out of the Whitney—I thought I recognized that coat, that cape, of yours? the red one?" Molly stares at Jenny and swallows hard and says, "Yes, well—I wasn't wearing it when I was in New York last week, and I didn't go to the Whitney. I guess you just confused Jonathan and me with someone else."

13 James says carelessly, "Why ask *me?*—he's the man with whom you live, after all."

"But Jonathan won't talk about it."

" 'It'—?"

"You. And him."

James smiles as if this information pleases him. "If my brother refuses to talk to you about me it's because he has always been obsessed with me." He pauses, lighting a cigarette. Molly waits to see the quick grimace that always accompanies the first lavish exhalation of smoke. "To be blunt; jealous of me."

"Jealous?"

"Pathologically."

"I can't believe that of Jonathan."

"Can't you?"

"He seems more—angry."

"Jealousy *is* anger. Suppressed rage."

"He has his own life, his own work—"

"And you."

Molly considers this. She can't judge the tone in which James has made the statement: ironic? envious? mock-envious? merely factual?

"I'm not sure," Molly says slowly, "that he wants me. I mean—completely."

James says nothing, perhaps he's bored. Molly dreads seeing him glance at his watch. She says, "He began to speak of you once—then grew quite agitated and stopped."

"Did he."

"And so I—I wondered."

89

"What did you wonder, Molly dear?" James asks. There's an edge to his voice so very like the edge to Jonathan's voice at certain tense moments that Molly has an impulse to clamp her hands over her ears.

She thinks, I must not ask.

She says, "I wondered why."

" 'Why'—?" James says coolly.

"He became so upset. I'd never seen him like that before and in a sense," Molly says, frowning, "—in a sense it all began then."

"Molly, don't be coy. *What* all began then?"

She looks at James helplessly thinking, you.

She says, confused, dropping her eyes, "I can't explain."

"Yes you can, love," says James, reaching for her. "If you try."

But another time when Molly brings up the subject—as if casually—James is surprisingly receptive. In high spirits (quite literally: he has treated himself and Molly Marks to some very fine-grade cocaine) he seems quite willing to talk about Jonathan, to a degree. Perhaps the subject amuses him?

"First of all, I want to make it plain that there is no 'animosity' between my brother and me, as you seem to believe. For how can there be animosity between us when it isn't shared? I assure you *I* feel no animosity toward him. I rarely think of him at all. People do, now and then, it's true, mistake me for him—as they must mistake him for me—but it really goes no further than that. Sometimes mutual acquaintances stop me on the street and, when they discover I'm Jonathan's older brother, ask me about him—and I'm perfectly civil, I'm perfectly friendly. I— Why do you look so unusually obtuse, Molly? Did I say something that puzzles you?"

"You spoke of yourself as Jonathan's 'older' brother."

"Well—I am older, technically, by about eleven minutes."

"Eleven minutes!"

"Which does make me older, doesn't it? Why are you smiling like that?"

"Eleven minutes doesn't seem, well, like very much,"

Molly says. She sees, uneasily, that James has not meant to be amusing. The man is dead serious. "It just doesn't—seem like very much."

"It may not seem like very much to you but it's a matter of public record—the hospital's records, and our birth certificates. I was born eleven minutes before Jonathan and I was born head first, whereas Jonathan's birth was more difficult. Very nearly a breech birth. My mother had had a long and arduous labor and while delivering Jonathan she lost a good deal of blood. At birth I weighed five pounds two ounces and Jonathan weighed just under five pounds. From the very first—I mean, in the womb, and perhaps at the literal instant of conception—I was the dominant twin. I'm sure Jonathan has neglected to tell you *that.*"

This proud and rather impassioned speech astonishes Molly, who has never heard James McEwan speak in quite this manner. She says, "In fact I think he did. He said something about your being 'dominant' in certain situations—in school, mainly—because he allowed you dominance. Because he didn't care."

James laughs luxuriously. "That's amusing! *That's* a revelation! 'Because he allowed me dominance.' 'Because he didn't care.' " He gets abruptly to his feet and begins to pace, smiling happily. The air turns turbulent in his wake. "What a joke! I'm delighted you're telling me this! I would have surely thought that, aged thirty-six, the man had progressed beyond his adolescent fixation on me, and his really quite embarrassing rationalization of my 'dominance' and his 'subordination.' These are facts of science, these are medical facts, hardly to be contested. It seems my brother even now finds it intolerable to accept himself as second, as inferior, as a mere epigone—" James rubs his hands together energetically; it might almost be that Jonathan, poor Jonathan, is close by, an unwitting witness.

Molly says quickly, "I just can't believe that of—"

"His pride! His pathological-paranoid pride!"

"—the fact that you *are* twins—"

"Yes but *are* we twins, in the conventional sense of the word?" James asks. He is calmer now; sits beside Molly on

the sofa (they are in the living room, no lights burning so
that the twilit glimmer beyond the wall of windows irradiates
into the room, chill, pale, romantic); grips her hand hard.
"If the two of us were literally identical, precise mirrors of
each other, *he* wouldn't be consumed with jealousy; to what
purpose would he be jealous? The galling thing for Jonathan
is that we are *not* identical."

"No," says Molly slowly, wondering if she is betraying
Jonathan, "I suppose not."

"Except in certain technical details. For instance, I.Q. Did
he tell you about our I.Q.?"

"No," says Molly.

"It's rather odd, and I never fully understood it, but when
we were tested as children—and we underwent a battery of
tests, my parents were suckers for this sort of thing—our
I.Q.'s always turned out precisely the same. Up a point or
two, down a point or two, we matched each other, invariably.
The last time we were tested, our senior year in prep school,
we were both 157—which seems high for Jonathan, doesn't
it? In the 'genius' range after all." James laughs, shaking his
head in disbelief. "But the really odd thing was how the
I.Q.'s always matched, no matter if one of us was deliber-
ately careless, or left out a question, or wasn't feeling well.
We were suspected of cheating though no one could figure
out how we were cheating since they tested us in different
rooms. One psychologist was convinced we were sending
extrasensory messages to each other—which we were assuredly *not.*" James pauses, lighting a cigarette. He's clearly
agitated, excited. Molly thinks she has never seen him so . . .
like Jonathan. "I don't believe in that sort of claptrap. ESP
and 'psychic communication.' It may have been that, as babies, when we were more obviously twins, we sucked each
other's thumb, as my parents claimed—*they* thought the dis-
gusting habit was cute!—and it's said we took turns crying
for my mother. Many, if not most, twins do such things—
even mere fraternal twins. Our parents claimed too that when
we first learned to crawl and then to walk it seemed to them
that one of us (probably me) advanced more quickly than the
other but that the other seemed to absorb his progress, so to

speak, and to match him within hours; so that there was a kind of osmotic transmission of motor skills. And that the same phenomenon took place when we began talking. *And* we had, like so many twins, a private language, a mimicry of adults' talk and some of our own code sounds—at least my parents said so. I remember nothing of that period of my life—it doesn't interest me in the slightest. I live in the present as I counsel my clients to live in the present because, if you look around, you'll see that's all there *is*—the present moment.''

Molly looks uneasily around. The long dreamy expanse of the living room, its shadowy corners so indistinct they seem to open out into the dusk. . . . She knows she should leave for Lindesfarne, it's already after six, but James's revelations fascinate her. If only he will keep talking! ''Then you don't think you and Jonathan ever shared any sort of special understanding?'' she asks cautiously.

''Has *he* indicated we have?''

''No.''

''*I* am revolted by the whole romance of twins, twinhood . . . the idea that two perfectly separate and individualized human beings are linked together psychically the way the Siamese twins Chang and Eng were linked together by a breastbone!'' James says contemptuously. ''Of course one twin is influenced by the other; and there are coincidences of a peculiar kind, often. But that isn't the same as a psychic connection.''

Molly says carefully, ''Doesn't it depend upon what you mean by 'coincidence'? I've read that—''

''For instance, Jonathan was always under my spell, so to speak, when we were children. He looked up to me as to an older brother; even when he resisted me, it was reactive—*his* response to *my* initiative. He even imitated my illnesses and accidents as if he couldn't bear to be left out. If he got sick, for instance, I usually remained well; but if I got sick, he came down with the illness within twenty-four hours. The summer we were ten, I fractured my ankle in a bicycl— cident, and a few weeks later *he* fractured his ankl bicycle accident. *It was precisely the same fracture,"* James says triumphantly. "Isn't that revealing!"

Molly, who remembers the account differently, murmurs in agreement.

"Jonathan was fully capable of making friends of his own— he was, and I'm sure still is, a quite charming person—but, no, he wanted *my* friends. He was always trying to attach himself to *my* popularity. If I joined a certain club Jonathan would join. When I ran for class president—this was at Well-come, our prep school, junior year—he allowed himself to be talked into running for vice-president, for the 'fun' of it. We both won. We both polled the same number of votes. And it was written up in our local newspaper—the sort of cute twin-kitsch that does get written up. Why will people persist in thinking twins are *cute!*—it's as perverse, I've always thought, as their thinking, in the past, that twins are *monsters.* You know of course, or maybe you don't know, that some prim-itive and some not-so-primitive peoples used to kill the second-born of a twin set?—the second-born being, usually, underdeveloped and puny, unlikely to thrive. The first-born or dominant twin absorbs more nourishment in the womb; in some rare cases," James says, laughing, squeezing Molly's hand, "—the dominant fetus *absorbs the smaller fetus* in the womb, and what was to have been a twin brother winds up a fossilized sort of tumor in the remaining twin! Think of that!"

Molly shudders, thinking of it. Her beloved Jonathan a mere growth in this man's big warm nerved-up body?

But she wants James to talk about Jonathan. She guides him back to his original topic, asking what it was like for them, as twins, to go to the same school. "I suppose there were pressures on you both?—to do equally well?"

"He may have felt pressure; I didn't. Studies came easily to me and if my grades weren't always invariably as high as Jonathan's during the school year—I was careless, cut classes, that sort of thing—I always made up for it at final examination time, by studying very hard, cramming weeks of work into a few days. Jonathan once claimed—I hope he was joking—that I benefited from his having worked seriously

because, when we took our exams, I could somehow read his mind and get the answers right, at least on true or false, or multiple-choice questions. It infuriated him that he, the 'good' McEwan, wound up with exactly the same grades as the 'other' McEwan. And there wasn't a thing he could do about it.''

Molly thinks, poor Jonathan!

''Of course it was my parents' fault, for sending us to the same school—the Wellcome School, up in Roxbury, New Hampshire. It's an excellent school, quite demanding, in fact, but Jonathan was at a disadvantage. He might have shone, *would* truly have shone, at another school. He's bright, immensely earnest, likeable—as you know. A bit of a prude, a puritan for work, but he could be rather fun at times, I'll admit. In sports—tennis, track, football—we were very nearly equals, if I practiced as I should have done, and taken it seriously. It was in social life that Jonathan had problems. His girlfriends invariably drifted in my direction and were reluctant to drift back in *his*. He had crushes on my girls but they weren't at all interested in him until—this happened so many times!—I lost interest in them; and then, abruptly, Jonathan lost interest too. I—''

James has been speaking rapidly and zestfully but he stops suddenly. As if he has just recalled something.

''—I think that's enough of the McEwan twins for the time being,'' he says, rather sharply. ''Don't you have to get back to *him?*''

14

"Here," says Jonathan, "—a surprise."

It isn't Molly's birthday and it isn't any holiday she knows of but quickly calculating as she unwraps the present—something rather chunky in a rectangular white cardboard box, elegantly gift wrapped—she realizes it is the third anniversary of their meeting: February 2. "—Something for the apartment, really," Jonathan says self-consciously. "I hope you like it."

Molly's pretty face has colored with pleasure, or with guilt, she doesn't deserve a present from Jonathan but she unwraps it excitedly just the same. "How nice of you," she says. "Dear Jonathan. How *sweet*."

Then she sees what it is—a carved jade figurine.

"Oh! it's beautiful," she says.

She stares at it, making no move to lift it from the box.

"Beautiful," she says faintly.

"I thought you might like it," Jonathan says, "—I thought, you know, it would suit your taste."

He takes it out of the box for her. It *is* beautiful—a finely carved big cat, a panther, about twelve inches long, with narrowed eyes and the most subtle suggestion of a snarl and a long graceful upward-curved tail.

"It's perfect," Molly says, her voice still rather faint.

Jonathan is clearly fascinated with the piece. He found it, he said, quite by chance in a Bridgeport antique shop the other day, actually he was just walking by and happened to glance in the window and there it was—and he knew it *was* perfect.

"I think you told me once, a couple of years ago, you were partial to jade," he says. "Didn't you?"

"Oh yes," says Molly, "—I am," says Molly, though she doesn't remember; and strongly doubts she ever said such a thing. Her liking, too, for jade is only recent.

15

James says, "I think you should plan to stay overnight in the city, Thursdays."

"I can't," Molly says, shocked. "—I have to work Friday mornings."

"Take the morning off, then. Your hours are flexible."

"I *can't*. What would I tell Jonathan?"

James looks at her as if she has said something both preposterous and in poor taste.

"—I suppose I could tell him I wanted to do things in the city," Molly says falteringly. "—see friends, or go to a play, or a lecture—"

"Why should you *tell* him anything?—you're a free agent," James says coolly.

Molly finds it difficult to look directly at James. His sleepy hooded eyes, the weight of his jaws, the powerful heat of his flesh—he is a presence, a force, that draws her to it even as she tries to resist. It's as if the very ground beneath her feet were tilted in his direction and all her conscious exertion is required to keep her balance.

"I—I might take a course at the New School," Molly says suddenly. "I mean—Jonathan would understand that. I mean I would *say* I was taking a course—"

"Columbia," James interrupts. "The quality of instruction is likely to be higher, and the university is closer to Dr. Wexler's office."

"And where would I stay?" Molly asks.

James laughs with pleasure, baring his teeth. As if Molly Marks has finally said something truly witty.

* * *

Molly waits for James to hint that he wasn't, isn't, serious, about her spending Thursday nights with him. But he behaves as if the subject is closed.

She says, "You know—I really don't think it's possible. Staying overnight in the city."

"And why is that, Molly love?"

"I—I would like to, but—"

"Yes?"

She cannot look at him. He stands squarely before her, smiling ironically. "There *is* my job," she says weakly, "and of course there's—"

"Yes?"

"—Jonathan."

"Ah. Yes. But what has he to do with it?—with us?"

"I don't know what I would tell him."

"You have already said what you would tell him."

"I—I don't know if I really want to be away from him that long," Molly says uncertainly. "He'd be alone—he might be lonely. He might think I didn't love him anymore." Her words shock her: she cannot bring herself to look up at James's face. "I mean—he'd be alone all those hours."

James laughs heartily, dismissively. "Darling," he says, kissing her goodbye, "you're a free agent—as you know. You must do what you want to do."

"Must I . . . ?" Molly Marks whispers.

16 On Valentine's Day Molly Marks is interviewed for the position of assistant to the director of the Lyndon Rees Foundation, headquarters in nearby White Plains. She learned of the opening by way of one of Jonathan's friends who knew from Jonathan she was looking for another—"worthwhile"—job. (Though it annoyed Molly that Jonathan had told the friend, and probably others. What if her current employers found out?) The Rees Foundation provides tax-free grants to individuals and organizations of an artistic and/or liberal nature—ecological studies, shelters for battered women and children, arts festivals, the sponsorship of a prisoners' literary magazine, an ACLU-sponsored tenants' union. (*"Grindingly* good," as James said, yawning, when Molly told him about the Foundation.)

This sun-bright midwinter morning Molly makes an excellent impression on the director and his several board members, neatly if rather schoolgirlishly dressed, hair tamed and face scrubbed and expression earnest, turning a ring on her finger in just the proper display of nervousness. She's smiling, eager, sensitive, intelligent . . . concerned with the "plight" of the poor, the need for "artistic expression" . . . of course she's a feminist. Enumerating the many college-level courses she has had in sociology, psychology, art history, English literature, American studies, she glides over the fact (so muffled, *is* it a fact?) that she hasn't technically a B.A. degree from Radcliffe . . . or elsewhere. And if she accepts this position she will take a substantial salary cut.

An hour later she telephones Jonathan at his office. "Good

news! I start work in two weeks!'' And Jonathan seems pleased—of course; *must* be pleased, for hasn't this been his idea from the start? His tone, however, is rather distant, distracted. He congratulates Molly and says they will have to celebrate that evening but it isn't possible for him to talk now and it isn't a very good idea, really, for her to call him at the office. Unless, he says, it's a genuine emergency.

So Molly, repentant, hangs up. And thinks of whom else she might call . . . ? Whom else, to tell her good news? Yes she has taken a salary cut and yes the job isn't quite as fast-paced or as glamorous or as lucrative as her present job but it has certain advantages of a moral kind. And of a practicable kind as well: she will be working only four days a week, with Fridays free.

17

Molly Marks thinks, calmly, I really don't want to see that man again.

It's a Friday morning in March, or is it already Friday afternoon. She's on the expressway speeding out of the city and she's wearing dark glasses against the snowy glare and her skin is pale, dense like milk gone sour. Eyes threaded with blood from not enough sleep and not enough nourishing sleep. And she recalls a nocturnal mirror-face dazed and grinning sporting watery blood-edged teeth. Is it, was it, possible? Her lower lip is pleasantly sore but not swollen.

James says, I *do* like you. You're *sweet.*

James laughs and says, You're so *funny,* Molly-Holly.

Jonathan says—shy, indirect, he's a master of indirection very like his brother—maybe it *is* time.

Time?

Maybe.

(They do, Molly Marks and Jonathan McEwan, use the expression "start a family" when they speak of certain matters. But Molly reasons that no one after all can overhear.)

How tender, tending his turtles. Which turtles have had offspring. Miniatures, as if carved: little baby-turtles Molly laughs at, they're so delightful. "How much beauty there *is* in the world, if only we know how to see it," Jonathan says passionately. It isn't his therapist voice and it isn't his husbandly voice, it's another voice Molly rather fears. Does he know her at all? she wonders. Seeing beauty after all in her. Face, body, "soul."

"—if we can only take time to see it," Jonathan amends.

102

His oracular statement has embarrassed him, there's only Molly Marks here, leaning against him, arm around his waist, head against his chest, snug.

"Oh Jonathan I love you so."

She's half sobbing and now *she* embarrasses him.

"Don't be silly, Molly," he says, laughing, delighted, not knowing what he says.

James says, Don't be stupid. Come here.

Do you like this? This? *This?*—Molly's voice but not one she recognizes. Rising to a near-scream. Then to a scream.

James says steering her in the direction of a Broadway-and-42nd-Street tattoo parlor (which, in her swaying drunk state, she mistakes at first for a porn shop—some of the tattoo illustrations are so graphic), "Let's get tattooed! The lady first!"

"Oh no," says Molly, shaking her head. "Oh no no no no *no.*"

"Yes," says James, "—I rather like this: the Sacred Heart of Jesus in full color. Or this: the American eagle in all his glory."

"Oh no," says Molly, laughing. She sees the man with the needle staring at her, he's got a lumpy face like cheese, swollen eyelids, hair that seems to ooze out of his skull, thin ropy oily strands. "Oh *no,*" says Molly, her voice rising, *"—noooooooooo."*

She's such a gorgeous girl. Everyone in the place is watching.

"I think we prefer words to images," James says severely. "If you'll excuse me, sir, some of your images are a bit . . . tacky."

"I don't want anything!" Molly says. "Not me!"

"The lady wants *James* in elegant script, inside one of those little hearts," James is saying, "—on, let's say, her derriere. How quickly can you do it, and what will it cost? Is your needle sanitary?"

The men are conferring and Molly hears herself laughing

though there isn't, is there, anything to laugh about. James is gripping her wrist hard and the tattooist is regarding her with a look of contempt so extreme as to be almost solicitous.

Molly's eyes snatch at his. She's shaking her head no, no, no, violent and despairing as a child.

Abruptly the tattooist rises from his stool and makes a spitting gesture. Says, "Get out of here, you two, we don't do stuff like that—go across the street." James says, "Suppose *I* want to be tattooed?" But the tattooist is walking away, the tattooist has dismissed them, Get the hell out of here you two he's mumbling, we don't do stuff like that.

James calls cheerfully over his shoulder, "We'll come back another time!"

No, Molly Marks thinks calmly, exiting at the Lindesfarne ramp—never.

18 Jonathan McEwan is teaching, not taking, an academic course this semester: a graduate seminar for the Yale psychology department in the principles of humanistic psychotherapy. It's just a coincidence of course, that Molly signed up for *her* course at Columbia (a course so vague as to shift its subject from week to week: "Social Interaction and Influence" plagiarized out of a university catalogue) at about the time that Jonathan agreed to take over a friend's course at Yale. He loves to teach, he says, but it wears him out—it's more draining, even, than doing psychotherapy.

Jonathan has seemed enthusiastic, at least to a degree, about Molly's rather sudden decision to take a night-school course this semester. Though surely he wonders why Columbia University and not somewhere closer, why a night in New York City apart from him. But he doesn't seem to be jealous or resentful. He doesn't *seem* to mind. "I'll miss you," he said sadly. "This place will be terribly empty without you."

But he quickly reverts to his former schedule on Thursdays: seeing clients through the afternoon and into early evening, then having a quick meal at a local restaurant (or so Jonathan says: in fact the man rarely eats alone, and rarely in restaurants, his friends' wives are delighted to cook for him on bachelor nights).

"You won't miss me at all," Molly says, hugging him close.

"Well—it *is* only one night a week," says Jonathan.

19 One night in early April Molly dreams again of the egg-smooth face. No eyes . . . no nose . . . no mouth—just a mask of skin. And behind it, inside it, a living being.

Except: the eye-indentations are a little more clearly defined than they have been, in other vaguely remembered dreams. And the mouth, though just a hairline crack, seems . . . more like a human mouth.

She doesn't tell Jonathan, she would never tell James, oh never.

Silly little twat with a silly little twat's dreams. Isn't that it? Why take yourself so seriously?

Lying awake covered in perspiration as after lovemaking and as nerved-up, trembling. Just a dream after all and it means nothing. Just a dream and what is a dream but wisps of surrealistic nonsense, the very worst of Dali (as James says of his clients' dreams), riddles without solutions, psychic teases. Jonathan urges his clients to speak of those dreams that have aroused strong emotion in them and to let the others go. Remembered in consciousness dreams are clearly not "dreams" any longer but something else, little narratives upon which the dreamer tries to impose meaning, significance. "How do they differ, then, from life?" Molly asked. Jonathan smiled, startled, as if Molly had said something meant to be amusing. And didn't answer her question.

20 "I don't like those people and I don't want to see them again," Molly says in a hoarse voice.

Driving with James in his metallic-black BMW along a near-deserted Tenth Avenue at two in the morning, rain-glittering pocked pavement and they've been quarreling, or as close to quarreling as Molly dares come, with James.

"I won't see them again," Molly says.

Balling a used Kleenex in her fist, dabbing her smudged eyes.

"You can't make me see them again," Molly says.

The wide wet avenue is empty of vehicles except for lone careening taxis. Northbound, southbound. Molly's throat is raw—feels like sandpaper. Her nasal passages are numb as if shot with Novocain.

They are as close to quarreling as Molly can recall except James isn't quarreling, that isn't his style. She has felt the flat of his hand and the nudge (playful, warning) of his fist and she knows better because it's two in the morning and raining and James is speeding up Tenth past Thirty-Seventh, Thirty-Eighth, Thirty-Ninth Streets running red lights or anticipating green lights, he's the kind of driver (somewhat like Jonathan in this respect, at more cautious speeds) who doesn't like to modify the pressure of his foot on the gas pedal, and still Molly persists, Molly says, "I hate you," Molly is screaming suddenly, "Let me out of the car God damn you, fuck *you,*" and James brakes the BMW to so abrupt a stop Molly is thrown forward against the dashboard.

James, imperturbable, leans across her to open the door.
It's a block of shuttered shops, darkened doorways, garbage
cans, litter. "We never do anything, dear girl, contrary to
your will."

And Molly hurtles herself out of the car. And the car speeds
away.

And away.

"I think it's making me worse," Molly tells Jonathan. "I
think it's making me have thoughts I would not ordinarily
have—like stirring up mud." She smiles strangely. "Muck."

"That's the principle of it, in a sense," says Jonathan.

He leans over her and kisses her lightly but she doesn't
seem to notice. She's staring out the window at the rain or
staring at the rain as it pelts the window, entranced, oddly
content, though there is an edge of bitterness in her voice.
There's amusement too. She says, "I'm thinking of not going
back."

"Not going *back?*" Jonathan asks. He's as surprised,
Molly thinks, as if she wanted to break off seeing him.

"Why? Is that wrong? Is something wrong with that?"
Molly says irritably.

"You don't just quit therapy on a whim, Molly."

"I don't intend to quit it on a whim!"

"This is the first time you've even mentioned quitting.
You've been seeing Dr. Wexler for how many months?—since
November?—and suddenly you want to quit? Why?"

"I don't know. I don't like her."

"I thought you did like her."

"I like her—the wrong way."

Jonathan stiffens. "What do you mean by that?"

"I like her too much. I mean, I want to please her too
much. I *don't* like her, I really hate her, but I wind up thinking about her all the time. I want to think," Molly says plain-
tively, "about you."

Jonathan laughs and kisses her again. "As I said, honey,
it's the principle of therapy—stirring up buried feelings. My
clients go through the same thing. I'm sure they hate me, and
some of them love me, and they think about me too much—

about 'Dr. McEwan,' in any case—and naturally they resent that. But you wouldn't be making any progress, Molly, if you didn't have these feelings.''

''Wouldn't I,'' Molly says.

''You owe it to yourself to keep trying, at least to go back for a few more sessions,'' he says gravely. ''And you owe it to your therapist.''

''Do I!'' Molly says, sighing.

She opens her damp crumpled Kleenex and blows her nose. Her head feels as if it's stuffed with cotton batting, or mucus.

21 Molly Marks's mother has disappeared!

She realizes, while lunching in White Plains with some newly made women acquaintances, and the subject of mothers-and-daughters comes up, that she has not fantasized her mother as a witness to her life for some time.

So she *is* cured, Molly thinks, amused. Of something, at least.

22

Molly says carefully, "I think I'm pregnant. I mean—I'm fairly certain I'm pregnant. I should know in another few days."

"Does *he* know?"

"That I'm waiting for the lab report? No."

"Why not? Don't you share such things?"

"I think," Molly says, and there's a long pause, "—I didn't want to frighten him."

"But *he* wants a baby too. Didn't you tell me he did?"

"Yes. I guess he does."

"Poor Molly-Dolly, you sound so wistful."

"Do I?"

"I love you when you're wistful. That pouty sulky disappointed look."

"Why do you say I look disappointed?" Molly asks, staring at him. "Of course I'm not disappointed."

"If you want to have a baby, and you say you do, you should be happier, shouldn't you? Really quite radiant?—as if something creamy and delicious were injected just under your skin? I love pregnant women—up to a point."

"Thank you," says Molly, her voice heavy with sarcasm.

"You seem to take him awfully seriously," says James. "To worry about, to seem in fact quite apprehensive of, *his* reaction. He—or I—only provided the sperm after all. Set the clockwork in motion."

Molly says nothing. She has a strong urge to hide her face in her hands.

James says, still in his playful cavalier tone, "Freud tells us that romantic love is the 'overvaluation of the individual'

111

but *we* know, don't we, dear, that Freud was a pig. Jung with all his wild lush poetic mysticism—his lifelong infatuation with the feminine—is rather more to our liking. Think of yourself as my brother's Anima: shifting from the archetype of the maiden to that of the mother. Perhaps it's time, you're pushing thirty.''

Still Molly says nothing. She feels inert, sluggish; like an organism of an indeterminate species, a jellyfish perhaps, floating and bobbing and dipping and slap-sucking on the surface of some stalled, brackish water. Not the proprietress of the organism but the organism itself: Molly Marks, pregnant at last!

"I feel as if I'm pushing thirty, all right," Molly says wryly. "Thirty of something heavy."

James laughs as if she has said something worthy of laughter though Molly knows better; but at least the man is making an effort to be kind. (As, always unexpectedly, he sometimes makes an effort to be sweet, or thoughtful, or tender, or even concerned for her . . . decent in the way that Jonathan McEwan is decent virtually all the time, with no visible effort.) Molly is sitting kimono-clad, bare-legged and -footed, on the edge of the gorgeous white sofa, hair spilling into her face, a warm vague retreating sensation, hardly more than a pulsebeat now, in her loins. Post-coital blues, pre-pregnancy blues except of course if she's pregnant she *is* pregnant. The laboratory report won't alter that.

Molly rouses herself and takes a swallow of her drink but discovers that the ice cubes have melted, the liquid has warmed, clamped between her moist palms. "Shit," she whispers.

James touches her shoulder, pokes her a little. "Are you worried, dear, that the baby might be mine?—because, if you are, I am not. A baby is your affair exclusively. I have a policy in such matters and I never swerve from it, you can depend upon me. If a woman elects to keep a baby whose father I might be, or, quite conclusively, am, it's her option; her affair," James says, not unkindly. "In any case, Jonathan's and my genes are identical. So there can be no problem about heredity—an infant who clearly embarrasses his father by not looking in any way like him, or behaving in any way like him. But all this, Molly, you know. All this," he says shrewdly, giving her another, sharper poke, "you must have been contemplating."

Molly looks up at him, unsmiling. "What is the secret between you and Jonathan?" she asks. "I want to know. Now."

"There is nothing 'between' us, as I've tried to explain," James says patiently. "Whatever absurd feelings he has about me are his affair; I assure you I don't share in them."

"But something happened between you. You *did* something to him."

"Is that what he says? If so, he's a liar. I did nothing contrary to his wishes, I assure you."

"What did you do?"

"When?"

"Ten years ago."

"Why must it be 'ten years ago'? Why not twenty, why not twenty-five, thirty-six?—at the moment of conception?" James says, laughing irritably.

Molly says, "Please tell me. I won't ask you anything more."

"Haven't you asked *him?*"

"Yes but he won't tell me."

"Tell him you'll trade his secret for your own."

"My own? What do you mean?" Molly asks. "I don't have any secret."

"Really, Molly!" James laughs.

"I mean—out of my past," she says, confused. "I mean anything of substance."

"What makes you think this is anything of substance?"

"Did you betray him in some way? Ridicule him in some way?"

"Why for Christ's sake do you go on about him!" James says. "One would think he occupied a central position in both our lives."

"Jonathan *is* your brother."

James laughs. "Shall I pour us a little more vodka, Molly

dear? And then you had better get dressed. And better, I think, be on your way home to suburban Connecticut."

"Why does he hate you so?"

"Molly, what a question to ask *me!* Ask him," James says, "—since it's his infantile emotion you're obsessed with."

"He wants me to marry him. I mean he has indicated he thinks we should get married—since there's no reason not to. And now," says Molly, choosing her words carefully, "if I am pregnant—"

"You really do seem morbidly attached to him," James says meanly. "Jonathan the second-born. Second-best."

"Jonathan isn't second-best."

"But of course he *is.* Do you think him first-rate? *Him?* Nobody knows your lover more intimately than I do, I assure you. I know him from the inside—in a sense I *am* him—but also, in addition to him, myself. Because I encompass my younger brother and I've gone beyond him—his limits, limitations."

"I don't understand you," Molly says, frightened. "What are you talking about?"

"How can I explain more clearly? I am Jonathan McEwan; but I am also James, who is more intelligent, more intuitive, more experienced; larger-souled, you might say. Come, Molly Marks, you must know this!—you *must* sense it. Otherwise why are you here, with me? And not there, with him?"

"I—just don't believe you," Molly says. "I don't want you to say such things."

"But Jonathan's psyche is transparent as gossamer, and no less flimsy! He hides his paranoia under a mask of Christly hypocrisy. He hides his pathological jealousy of his older, dominant brother—his jealousy of all superior men—inside a pose of generosity, fair-mindedness, *goodness.* What you have taken for Jonathan McEwan's personality is really just his *persona*—a partly conscious and partly unconscious mishmash of traits he'd like to possess, or be credited with possessing. All a pathetic self-dramatization, Molly, as you'll one day discover. And perhaps very soon."

James speaks rapidly, unsparingly. Molly has never heard

words quite like these in her life. She says, faltering, "You—you hate him and you're slandering him. It's—"

"I don't slander," James says coldly. "As I told you—I don't lie."

"I don't believe these things about Jonathan!" Molly says angrily. She sets her glass on the coffee table but it slips from her wet hands and falls to the floor. And, seeing it fall, Molly kicks at it—gives a high-pitched little scream and kicks. She's on her feet beating her fists against her thighs screaming at James. "You're lying—you *do* lie—you *do* lie about your brother! I should tell him the terrible things you say!"

James wipes at his trousers with a tissue, seemingly unperturbed. Though Molly can see that the edges of his mouth have gone white; as do Jonathan's, when he's upset.

"Tell him? Go ahead, Molly. Tell him what you will."

"I think you're really jealous of *him.*"

James shrugs.

"I think you're really obsessed with *him.*"

"Go home, Molly Marks. You can find your own way out."

"I don't even think," Molly says, backing down a little, "that you know him. Any longer. As he is now. The way I know him."

But James is looking at her with genuine distaste. "Go home, go home. Get dressed and go home. You seem to have suddenly—rapidly—lost your looks. And all your charm depended upon them."

Molly stands forlorn, frightened, staring at James McEwan. She has seen Jonathan angry as this but never James. The man's blood-dark heavy face is closed like a fist; the cheeks bunched as with muscle; the eyelids finely trembling. She knows that, if she dared touch him, she would feel the tension quivering through his body.

"If you really want me to leave—"

"I do."

"—then I will."

She runs into the bedroom, she slams into the bathroom, and though she hasn't heard him and could not have believed how quick, and how silent, he is, there he is close behind her—his face contorted with rage. She raises her arms to protect herself and he brushes them away. He slaps her face, open-handed—one side and then the other—knocks her back against the wall, against a mirror that, dislodged, almost crashes to the floor. "Bitch. Cunt. *Stupid* cunt," James whispers.

He drags her back into the bedroom. And later, when Molly is sobbing, hiding her face in the pillow to muffle her sobs, he says, "Now do *go* before I really lose my temper. Do, do *go.*"

23 By the time the laboratory report comes in—yes: positive: Molly Marks *is* pregnant—it has all become irrelevant. A moot point, Molly tells herself, not bitterly but merely practically, dealing with the unusually heavy discharge of menstrual blood she's enduring this time; home from work for two days, with severe cramps, nausea, a blinding but somehow soothing headache—doped up with codeine, which she rather likes. Now her head *is* cotton batting and it suits her.

And all this suffering not altogether beyond the periphery of Jonathan McEwan's tender concern . . . though of course Jonathan thinks it is nothing more serious than the usual affliction, tuned a bit higher.

He brings her herbal tea as she lies in bed, or on the living room sofa; heats up some Campbell's chicken gumbo soup, one of Molly's favorites from her bachelor girl days. He's sweet, solicitous, vaguely embarrassed like any husband, lover, boyfriend, boy. "Poor Molly," he says, laying the flat of his hand against her stomach, "—but it won't last long. You'll be up and around before you know it." His hand is burning; Molly loves it there; Molly wants it never to be removed.

But she knows better than to let things get too solemn. She knows the value of a joke at such moments. "Just an excuse to take off from work," she says. "To cancel out with Wexler this week," she says, smiling wanly.

But prettily: papery paleness becomes Molly Marks.

PART
THREE

24 It is in June, nearly a full calendar year to the day after Molly Marks and Jonathan McEwan moved into their apartment on the seventh floor of Greenwood Towers, that the telephone call comes: mere coincidence of course. The phone rings at 11:45 A.M. and Molly picks up the receiver. "Hello," she says brightly, half hoping it's for Jonathan and not for her since this is a Saturday morning awash in Saturday chores and errands, the kind of morning when nothing serious or significant or very likely diverting will happen, she's in a sweatshirt and blue jeans, barefoot, damp hair drying on her shoulders and no makeup and her skin feels scrubbed, tight, innocent as a girl's. "Hello?" she says in her efficient telephone voice already sensing who it might be, what it might mean. She has not heard from James McEwan in approximately eight weeks but she has been thinking of the man more or less constantly, an undercurrent in her life, a dull pulsing ache like a bad tooth, she's been waiting for something to happen and now, "Hello, Molly Marks," comes the voice, familiar, intimate, mocking as her own interior voice, now it's happening. "How's everything in suburban Connecticut?"

Jonathan is typing in his study at the other end of the apartment and Molly is in the kitchen, leaning against the doorframe. She says faintly, "I—I can't talk to you now."

"Is *he* there?"

"No. I mean yes—he's here. He's home." Molly feels a wave of panic, seasickness. She says hurriedly, "I can't talk now, I have to hang up. I don't have anything to say to you."

121

"We haven't seen each other in some time, love. I've been missing you."

Molly shuts her eyes. Draws a deep shuddering breath and prepares herself.

"Haven't you been missing me?"

"No."

"Molly dear, don't be coy. Haven't you?"

"I don't want to see you again. I don't want to talk to you."

"I can quite understand that you don't want to see me again, that you're anxious about—*are* you pregnant?"

"Yes."

"—about being pregnant and settling down with my brother; trying to make the best of the situation. The best of second-best but we won't go into *that*—I know you're sensitive about it." James pauses. Molly imagines she can hear him breathing. "Molly? You have been missing me, haven't you?—saying you don't want to see me again is not quite the same thing as saying you haven't missed me, after all."

"I'm going to hang up," Molly says. "I'm through with all this."

"What did you tell him?"

"I don't want to *talk* to you. I hate you."

"Yes of course, that's to be expected. But you like me too so coyness is beside the point. What did you tell *him?*"

"What do you mean? When?" Molly asks. Her eyes dart about the gleaming kitchen, nowhere to rest. She's weak-kneed, her heart thumping hard and quick in her chest. Why has he called?—why today?

"About your 'therapist,' and the rest. We've been out of contact a long time."

"I said I'd quit. I'd had enough."

"So you don't come to New York City quite as frequently?"

Molly makes a laughing snorting sound.

"You disappoint me," James says, offended. "You sound crude and insensitive and not at all like the Molly Marks I adored."

You bastard, Molly thinks.

"You disappointed me that night, and you disappoint me now. Don't you think you owe me something?"

"Are you crazy? Owe *you* something?"

"Of course. You know very well what I mean."

"After what you did? You—"

"After what *you* did. Let's get that straight."

Molly says, pleading, "Why are you doing this? I told you—I'm pregnant—" She drops her voice, reiterating the lie. She can still hear the undertone of Jonathan's typing.

"I told you I quite adore pregnant women, up to a point," James says. "You have months to go before that point."

"You just want to hurt us. To hurt Jonathan."

"He has nothing to do with it, I assure you," James says, annoyed. When Molly says nothing he adds, *"I* want to see you again, this week. Shall we resume Thursdays?"

"Are you crazy?"

"Thursdays, same time, same place?"

Molly thinks, He *is* crazy.

"I'm through with all that," Molly says hurriedly. "I'm going to hang up now."

"Because you're going to have a baby?—the baby that might in fact be *ours?*"

Molly has forgotten that. She has forgotten all that and now she says angrily, not quite coherently, "It isn't. I was lying. It isn't anything of yours!"

"Same time, same place? Next Thursday?"

"It isn't anything of—"

"Goodbye, love!"

And James McEwan hangs up.

And Jonathan McEwan is saying, "Molly? Who was that? Is something wrong?"

Jonathan has come up behind Molly without her having heard.

She gives a little start, seeing him. For here is James McEwan too—looming above her, big-bodied, big-headed, those staring hooded eyes, the heavy jaws with their perpetual bluish cast. "Nothing is wrong," Molly says quickly. She smiles, she's an expert at inventing quick plausible lies.

"Someone from the Foundation—a minor emergency but now I think it's cleared up."

Jonathan believes her of course for why would he not believe her?—though seeing her look of fright, apprehension, perhaps a little guilt, she's clever enough to turn it into a light amusing and of course plausible anecdote, something he'll listen to without needing to exactly hear, or remember. He's back at work in a minute and Molly remains in the kitchen leaning weakly against one of the counters, head bowed, hair falling forward . . . She cannot feel more agitated, more intimidated, if James McEwan had appeared at their door. If he'd slammed open the door and walked right in.

25

"Do you want to . . . try again? Keep trying?"

Jonathan's voice so gentle, so solicitous, Molly doesn't at first register the *you*. And after they make love she isn't in a state to recall it let alone interpret it.

Jonathan McEwan is the least suspicious of men and Jonathan believes her, of course. About starting therapy with the mythical Agnes Wexler, about stopping therapy ("I simply felt I'd learned all I needed or wanted to know about myself"), about dropping the night-school course. Those many weeks, those months, he has believed her or has not given her any reason to think he doesn't believe her, absorbed in his work, his professional career, the many people, men and women both, who constitute Jonathan McEwan's complex life apart from her. Molly is sometimes, Molly is fairly frequently, jealous of *him;* or, perhaps, jealous for him. As she is, still, for why not admit it?—jealous of, and for, James McEwan.

She thinks, If only he were dead!

Same time, same place? the son of a bitch said complacently but Molly Marks doesn't make the trip to New York City of course. And Molly Marks doesn't telephone of course. (Nor does James telephone her. Though she's in a virtual sweat of anxiety for days anticipating the call. Each time the telephone rings . . . her heart stops.)

* * *

This is what you deserve, Molly thinks.

Those many weeks, those months, and Jonathan was never
suspicious, making love with her only hours, sometimes, after his brother has made love with her, suspecting nothing
believing everything or so it seems. She wonders if she has
escaped with her life. She wonders if she *has* escaped with
her life.

She feels relief. And guilt—of course. And remorse.

And a subtle contempt?

It's a shameless lewd luxurious fantasy, adolescent if not
frankly juvenile, giving pleasure (of a kind) as such fantasies
do. It plays like a videotape brainlessly repeating itself as
Molly Marks commutes on the interstate to and from White
Plains, or showers, or prepares meals, wordless solitary ac-
tivities that free the imagination. . . . She acquires a gun
never mind how and she goes to him never mind how and
she shoots him in the heart or better yet in the groin: Take
that! Only St. Ives as a witness.

That is, Danton.

The fantasy quickly becomes so routine, it loses its edge.
Molly yawns. How do you acquire a gun, in any case?

Molly Marks doesn't go to New York and fully intends
never to see James McEwan again but, making love with
Jonathan, eyes shut tight, her slender body coiled like a
spring, she often catches herself thinking of . . . James; seeing in her mind's eye not Jonathan whom she loves but James
whom she detests; hearing James's low insidious mocking
voice in her ear. She clutches Jonathan in terror of crying out
James's name. She would suck Jonathan deep, deep into her,
would swallow him up, speaking his name as if he were an
incantation *Jonathan Jonathan Jonathan* . . . until she loses
all consciousness of what she does, and what she is trying
not to do.

26 Planning their August vacation, a leisurely drive up along the coast, up into Maine and perhaps into Nova Scotia if Jonathan can spare the time, if Jonathan doesn't get restless as he frequently does, away from work, away from his clients, Molly closes her fingers in his hair and gives his head a shake, Molly teases saying, "Does Dr. McEwan have a Savior-complex?—oh no!" which makes Jonathan blush and doesn't seem to antagonize him though a moment later Molly will feel a *frisson* of something like panic. Why has she said such a thing?

As if *he* were whispering in her ear.

But Jonathan isn't antagonized, Jonathan is too sweet-natured. He takes it as the harmless quip it's meant to be; doesn't even take it (as, surely, he'd be within his rights to) as a pushy wifey naggy remark meaning, Why aren't I enough for you? Meaning, maybe, Aren't I enough for you?

"Don't you have a summer place here? Narragansett?" Molly asks Jonathan, looking up from the map of New England, "—on the Rhode Island coast?"

Jonathan says, frowning, "Who told you that? Did I tell you that?"

For a terrible moment Molly wonders if it was James who told her.

"I—I guess you must have. We drove by it once. You—"

"It's been sold," Jonathan says. "It isn't ours anymore."

"Oh I see," says Molly. "You didn't tell me that."

"It was sold a long time ago," Jonathan says. It's his false voice, his evasive voice, a voice in which lies are told but inadequately told.

He can't lie either, Molly thinks.

Of course she doesn't pursue the subject. She isn't going to pursue the subject. She considers, nearly five weeks after James McEwan's telephone call that morning, that she has escaped with her life.

27 "Jonathan—!"

Molly Marks looks up from her desk at the Rees Foundation to see, unannounced, unexpected, Jonathan McEwan standing in her doorway, about to knock on her opened door. It's mid-September, a blazing-bright day, nearly noon, and Jonathan has come to take Molly to lunch if she's free, doesn't have a meeting . . . ? "I hope I haven't disturbed you," he says. He appears rather self-conscious, shy, almost a bit ungainly, in this new setting where he's out of place, glancing around Molly's cramped office as if, seeing it at last, he wishes it were more impressive. Molly jumps up and hugs him around the waist and kisses him. She assures him he isn't disturbing her, she's delighted to see him. She lowers her voice so that no one passing her doorway might overhear. "What a lovely surprise, Jonathan!" she says happily. "I was just thinking of you."

She has a few minutes' work to attend to so Jonathan waits for her outside, sitting on a ledge overlooking the quadrangular mall adjacent to the Foundation's headquarters, it isn't quite true that Molly is free for lunch but this is a special occasion and she isn't going to sabotage it. Jonathan has promised to drop by her office for months but has always been too busy.

"This is all very attractive," Jonathan says as they cross the mall hand in hand. He's looking hard at the potted trees, the mosaic-tile fountain, the flashy tiers of spouting water. "You're really quite fortunate to work here." "Oh—I've told you how I feel," Molly says. "Still," says Jonathan, meaning to be encouraging, perhaps, "it *is* an attractive setting." He's still somewhat self-conscious, stiff, Molly attributes it to his feeling out of place here and his worry about having intruded in her professional life, she's in too benign a mood she's simply too happy to notice or absorb the significance of certain incongruous details: the fact that Jonathan is wearing sunglasses with metal and not black plastic rims, the fact that he's wearing them at all since he wears them rather infrequently, and his sports coat is a lighter shade of brown than it should be, and his trousers, and his shoes, those aren't shoes Molly has seen Jonathan wear before but they do look familiar and she simply isn't thinking, poor silly twat, her arm now linked tight through his and she's chattering happily if a bit nervously though she could not have said why she's nervous unless she attributes it to (for instance) the powerful emotion she feels in Jonathan's presence and felt at the sight of him so unexpected in her doorway, smiling at her, about to knock on her opened door and surprise her with his presence: "Molly? I've come to take you to lunch, I hope I'm not disturbing you?"

"Oh no," came Molly's voice, girlish, elated, "—oh no honey of course not."

Afterward Molly will think, Oh Christ how could I.

Molly Marks steers the man she believes to be her lover in the direction of a restaurant up the street, the only really good restaurant in the neighborhood, luxuriantly shadowy, cool, polished wood and brass and soft-spoken waiters and enormous gilt-stamped tasseled menus in French and he orders a bottle of good white wine for them which is a gesture he would not ordinarily make ("But this is a special occasion") and Molly falls in with the celebratory mood, Molly will do most of the talking until the masquerade ends some forty-five minutes later.

Not Jonathan McEwan whom she loves but James McEwan whom she detests and how could she be such a *fool* such an *asshole* Molly Marks will berate herself for days, for the remainder of her life, seeing again his sweet shy smile, his heavy-lidded eyes gazing at her with intense interest; with love. He's shrewd enough to feed her questions to keep her talking, animated, distracted; to block any questions she might have of him, or for him. From time to time he reaches over to squeeze her hand. He laughs at her witty remarks, her charming little stories.

"This is such a lovely surprise," Molly says, more than once. "You can't know how seeing you cheered me up."

The waiter brings their food and delicious food it is, Molly's right about the restaurant, "We should do this more often," the man she believes to be Jonathan says, adding, "Darling," and winking at her as if they share a joke. And there's a beat or two—or three—as Molly absorbs something in his voice that shouldn't be there, some slight sliding note of complicity, mockery, but of course she can't be certain and discounts it, but there's the wink, something lewd about the wink, what about the wink, has Jonathan McEwan ever winked at her in all their months of intimacy? No.

And would he call her darling, in quite that way . . . ?

Molly lowers her wine glass with trembling fingers. No. Yes. But no: it can't be. Sees now the slight curling contempt in his lips, the crude hilarity rising in her companion's face.

James McEwan: smiling openly at her now.

"You!" says Molly.

James is already on his feet as Molly scrambles to hers. He takes hold of her arm, forces her back down into her chair.

"Don't," he says in a warning voice. "Don't cause a scene."

Molly sits. She's mute, stunned. So humiliated so profoundly shocked she isn't even angry.

James speaks swiftly and with a nervy sort of conviction, guessing how close Molly is to hysteria. Sorry he

says to have deceived her but what other way has he he
says of seeing her and he has missed her, he says, he *has*
missed her, he says, and can't believe she hasn't missed
him.

He continues to grip her arm, hard. Holds her immobile.
The color is up in his face and his wicked eyes shine, elated,
triumphant, oh Christ how hilarious it is, "Your face, poor
Molly," he says, exploding in laughter, "—you should see
your face," and he can't help laughing even harder, crude
and hearty from-the-gut laughter that draws glances from
other patrons. Molly hides her face, which is burning, in
her linen napkin. Molly herself is sobbing, or is she laughing, has a brief attack of hiccups, such shame such humiliation she's wishing she had her little pearl-handled revolver,
the fantasy-revolver she carries in her handbag and will use
one day to shoot her seducer in his black black heart, or in
his groin. "You bastard," Molly whispers. "Oh you
fucker."

"Not so loud, love," James says, wiping at his eyes.
"Strangers will overhear and *not* understand."

By degrees James relaxes; trusts her enough to remove his
hand from her arm. He pours the last of the wine in her glass.
He asks should they share a second bottle of wine or would
Molly prefer to waste time sulking?

"Fucker," Molly whispers.

"The wine, then," says James, signaling for their
waiter.

But when they leave the restaurant and step out into the
bright blazing autumnal sunshine Molly has recovered suffi-
ciently to tell him no; she won't see him again.

James laughs and tells her she isn't serious. Of course she
will see him again. Of course they will be lovers again.

Molly shakes her head no, Molly is walking quickly away.
She has had too much wine and the food she ate lies heavily
in her stomach and there's a sick sour taste in her mouth, this
time she has really had enough.

James calls after her, "Try out the name Sandra Shearer
on him—'Sandy Shearer.' " A mean malicious voice but

when Molly looks around it's to see that he's smiling at her, his hand upraised in a rather formal farewell and the man might—again—be Jonathan McEwan whom she loves and not James McEwan whom she detests.

" 'Sandy Shearer,' " he says, "—try it out."

28 "You know, Molly, I never did get over to White Plains to see your office. . . . You invited me, didn't you, and I never got there."

It is early one morning a few days after James's visit. Jonathan, shaving, calls out to Molly in the bedroom, speaking with a peculiar urgency.

"Am I still invited? What about Monday of . . ."

Molly pretends not to hear. Quickly leaves the room hurrying barefoot to the kitchen to start the coffee.

Before they leave the apartment for work Jonathan brings up the subject again, as if recounting a dream-message incompletely understood. Molly invited him, he never got around to accepting the invitation, what about Monday of next week? "We could have lunch together somewhere," Jonathan says, inspired. "If you're free. If I'm still invited."

Molly says quickly, not meeting his eye, "It isn't very impressive, I'm afraid. My office. My work."

Molly says quickly, "I don't think I am free, Monday. And most of next week . . ."

She turns away so that Jonathan can't see her face. She doesn't, at the moment, care to see his.

"Well," says Jonathan, puzzled, hurt, "it isn't really a good time for me either."

Second-born, James murmurs slyly.
Second-best.

They are sitting down to a dinner Molly has taken some pains to prepare and naturally the telephone rings . . . as it

134

will ring two or three more times that evening . . . since
Jonathan won't have the answering service on when he's
home—"It seems somehow fraudulent"—and Molly sits at
the table her hands in her lap not eating because she's too
angry she's furious at Dr. McEwan who is so quick to answer
the summons of that fucking ringing and so eager to sympathize, to listen, to "hear out," so slow to break the connection as if he has forgotten by this time about Molly Marks
whom in theory he loves and who loves him, only him.
Sometimes the party who interrupts them is a "client" and
sometimes it is a "colleague" and Molly has come to wonder
if there is any significant difference.

"Which leech was it tonight?" Molly asks when Jonathan
returns to the table.

"Molly," Jonathan says reprovingly.

"Which deadbeat?"

"It's a matter of some urgency but it isn't a matter you
need to concern yourself with," Jonathan says, "—so let's
drop the subject. Please."

Molly has the sudden fierce impulse to drop a plate—
shatter it on the floor—but the joke might not be clear. The
candles' flames are already tremulous and quivering in the
wake of Jonathan's passage.

But she can't resist saying lightly, "Some of us think we're
Jesus Christ, don't we!"

Jonathan passes it off, Jonathan won't be drawn into a quarrel, not at the moment though, later, Molly knows it will
come later, that night as they undress or as they get into bed
or as Molly kisses him, closes her fingers in his hair, he'll
say softly, "That's the second time, at least, you've said that
recently, Molly, about Christ, you know, 'some of us think
we're Jesus Christ,' what exactly are you suggesting?" And
now it will be Molly's turn, frightened Molly's turn, not to
be drawn into a quarrel. Not now.

Sandra Shearer.
"Sandy" Shearer.
Molly has spelled out the name dozens of times, idly, ab-
sentmindedly, at her desk or during meetings or, evenings,

in the margin of a magazine she's reading and will toss into
the trash . . . just one close call when Jonathan wanted to
read the magazine before Molly tossed it out, a women's
magazine and Molly had assumed she was safe defacing its
white margins with *Sandra Shearer, "Sandy" Shearer*, idle
distracted doodling she hardly knows she does.

Check it out with him, James said, sneering, but Molly
isn't going to, Molly doesn't dare.

And then Jonathan's father dies. And Jonathan leaves
abruptly for Arizona. And Molly is alone in the apartment
for what is supposed to be about three or four days but turns
into twelve very long very lonely days ("All sorts of family
complications" Jonathan tells her over the phone, "—don't
ask") and she reasons it is one of the advantages of not being
a wife that, on such disagreeable occasions, she isn't obliged
to accompany her husband. And she reasons it is one of the
disadvantages too.

One night, late, she doesn't know why, doesn't intend to
talk to him but—she dials James McEwan's private number
in Manhattan. Of course he isn't there, she's referred to an
answering service and quickly hangs up. And next morning,
again not knowing why, she telephones his office and his
receptionist tells her that Dr. McEwan is out of town at a
relative's funeral and if she would like to leave her name and
number. . . . "No thank you," Molly says mysteriously,
meanly. "Once was enough."

Jonathan calls her, she hopes not dutifully, but certainly
promptly, at six each evening. "I'm lonely here," Molly says
wistfully, "—I miss you," Molly says, "—the apartment
doesn't seem right without you." Jonathan says rather
vaguely, "Yes of course," as if he hasn't been listening,
"—I miss you too." He seems distracted; a bit curt; rarely
stays on the line more than ten minutes. He tells Molly that
his father was eighty-three years old and had been in failing
health for years but the death seems to have unhinged his
mother temporarily just the same. He hopes, temporarily.

"I hope so too," Molly says.

(If it strikes Molly as odd, if it has struck her for some

time, as odd, that Jonathan McEwan evidently feels no urgency about introducing her to his family, she naturally says nothing. Jonathan's family is his affair just as her family is hers.)

Molly speaks with her father from time to time, on the phone. He knows she is "cohabiting" with a man but he will not pursue the subject and Molly isn't going to pursue it either. "As long as you know what you're doing," has been Mr. Marks's sour comment on his daughter's life for the past eleven years and Molly has always said cheerily, "Oh sure, Daddy—*I* know," and that's that. When, vague and apologetic, she tells Jonathan that it isn't quite the right time for him to meet her father yet, maybe when they've definitely set the date for the wedding, maybe then, Jonathan always agrees; Jonathan never objects. "Not that Daddy wouldn't like you very much," Molly adds hopefully. Jonathan says, "Yes I'm sure." And the subject is adroitly dropped.

The fifth day of Jonathan's absence Molly asks casually, "Your brother—is *he* out there too? Is *he* staying so long?"

Jonathan answers quickly, "No. Of course not."

There's a pause; clumsy blank silence.

"You mean he didn't come at all?" Molly asks, puzzled. Jonathan laughs and it's like ice being rattled, thinly, in a tray. He says, "My brother doesn't take family obligations quite as seriously as I do."

"I see," says Molly.

Though she doesn't, quite.

"He doesn't take *family* seriously," Jonathan adds.

"I—I'm sorry to hear that," Molly says.

Again there is a clumsy pause. Molly repeats, weakly, not knowing what else to say, "I'm sorry."

"Why should you be sorry?" Jonathan asks coldly. "It has nothing to do with you."

29 Sandra Shearer.
"Sandy."
There, in the Wellcome School yearbook, amid the dozen or so *S*'s of the graduating class of 1968. There, smiling up at Molly Marks, so pretty!—so very young!

And she has signed her name, exclamatory girlish red ink, *Dear Jonathan—Love Always, Sandy* noting the date 13 June 1968 and embellishing her two-by-three-inch photograph with a frame of intricately linked red hearts.

Of course it has been a long time, the red ink has seriously faded.

Molly swallows hard. *My God she looks like me* is a thought she discards almost at once. Because it isn't really true. Because the girl has a fuller face than Molly Marks did at seventeen; wears her hair differently, cut short, and Molly always wore hers long—still does. Because the girl is so pert and cute and determinedly sweet and she looks far more innocent than Molly did at that age. And far more vulnerable.

"So this is 'Sandy Shearer,' " Molly thinks.

For some reason her eyes fill with tears. Why?

She studies the young girl's picture, wishes it were in color. Brown hair? Brown eyes? Skin tone? Beneath the photo is the usual little boastful litany of credits—National Merit Society, president of Wellcome Glee Club, girls' intramural volleyball, Wellcome *Clarion* editorial staff, honors in English and French, etc. Smart, cute, popular. The usual. But why is it all so sad, Molly wonders. She has no reason to think the girl is dead.

She turns back to the *M*'s, locates *McEwan*, and here, shockingly, before she is quite prepared for it, is Jonathan's picture—and a neatly scissored out rectangle where James's had been.

Molly winces as if she has seen something forbidden. Has Jonathan always hated James so much? Or did he cut the picture out at a later date?

Jonathan is immediately recognizable though astonishingly young . . . just a boy, *so* young . . . his cheeks thinner, with something tentative about the mouth, eyes slightly narrowed as if anticipating the photographer's flash. A suggestion of acne on the forehead. A guarded little smile.

Molly studies the likeness, Molly thinks, yes, she would have been attracted to this boy as a young girl herself.

But: "Poor Jonathan," she thinks.

The space beside Jonathan is just that—empty space. No James McEwan. Even his caption is missing.

Molly looks through the yearbook half dreading what else she will find. And, yes, Jonathan has carefully scissored out James's picture several more times . . . while leaving his own untouched. In a group shot of the school newspaper staff Jonathan McEwan stands in the back row, a tall handsome husky boy, smiling tentatively at the camera, while beside him on his right is—an empty slot; a hole in the page. But, below, the identification remains untouched: *James McEwan.*

Such spite, thinks Molly. Such meanness.

She recognizes Sandra Shearer in this picture, a taller girl than Molly would have guessed. And very pretty, very sweet . . . at least to the casual eye. That level determined smile that does remind Molly of her own at that age. That utterly charming tilt of the head.

You want to be: lovable, and seductive; quick-witted, and sweet; popular, and brilliant.

You want: all you can get away with.

Molly presses her face against the yearbook's glossy pages and inhales deeply. That indefinable pungent smell . . . that unmistakable smell . . . of an old school yearbook no one has opened in a very long time.

* * *

Molly has done a risky thing, in Jonathan's absence, and will Molly regret it?

Like Pandora, opening the forbidden box!

She thinks it unlikely, however, that Jonathan will ever find out. She is careful to put everything back in the cardboard boxes—neatly wrapped, dated—in which she found them, and to stack the boxes precisely as they were in Jonathan's study closet. All very ordinary material, for the most part, nothing that would embarrass Jonathan (except the deletions in the yearbook and a few similarly mutilated snapshots) or call into question his moral integrity.

Personal papers, documents, files, elaborate student notes, hundreds of pages of notes in fact, typed and in longhand; torn manila envelopes stuffed with snapshots (disappointingly few) and news clippings (also few, evidently from Jonathan's hometown paper: *McEwan Twins Tie for Top Honors, McEwan Twins Score Identical Points in '66–'67 Wellcome Varsity Season, McEwan Twins Awarded Nat'l Merit Scholarships*). Most of Jonathan McEwan's personal things are impersonal, Molly thinks, or might belong to anyone.

Odd, so few letters from friends. And no love letters. If Jonathan received them, and surely he did, he wasn't sentimental about keeping them. It chills Molly to think that, if she and Jonathan broke up, he'd have no evidence of her either. Nor would she of him.

That night Molly sleeps poorly. Dreams of the nightmare skin-smooth face, and of Sandra Shearer's face, and of Molly Marks's own, faces carelessly shuffled together, like playing cards.

30

"Tell me anything you can about her," Molly says. "Just—anything."

So a Miss Riordan of the Alumni Affairs Office of the Wellcome School of Roxbury, New Hampshire, supplies some factual information about Sandra Shearer '68: her hometown was, or is, Fitchburg, Massachusetts; she maintained a 3.4 grade point average and graduated fourth, *magna cum laude,* in a class of seventy-five; she won a number of school awards and honors; received a National Merit Scholarship and went to Mt. Holyoke; seems not to have attended her tenth class reunion in 1978, and has failed to respond to various alumni mailings. . . . "But she *is* alive?" Molly asks anxiously.

Miss Riordan looks at Molly through the sharp-focused lenses of her glasses. "There is no record of her having died," she says. "Do you have any reason to believe she has?"

Molly Marks murmurs no, not really, she just hasn't heard from her old friend Sandra Shearer in a very long time.

Molly speaks with Mr. Muller, Headmaster of the Wellcome School, a brisk little man with a hard handshake, all smiles but a sharp eye and he seems at first suspicious of Molly Marks (is she writing a journalistic exposé of the school?—a piece for the *New York Times* on the preppy drug culture?) though he speaks directly enough, and means to be helpful: yes of course he remembers the girl, seems to remember her, though he could be describing, Molly thinks, any number of girls—honors student, school leader, serious hard-working reliable, in the classic tradition of the Wellcome School etcetera. Too many Sandys, thinks Molly. Too many of us. When Mr. Muller asks what Molly's interest is in the young woman Molly tells him what she told Miss Riordan and heads him off before he can ask another question (such as why Molly hasn't simply contacted her friend's family)—"Do you happen to remember, too, the McEwan twins, also of the class of 1968—Jonathan and James?" And Mr. Muller's expression shifts because now indeed he does remember. "Ah yes—James and Jonathan!" he says, shaking his head, "—of course I remember *them.*"

But his memory of James and Jonathan is cheery and benign and vague, they were excellent students they were hardworking students etcetera. . . . "Of course, being identical twins, they were always confused with each other," he says, "which could lead sometimes to . . . confusion."

In the red-brick Georgian English Building Molly speaks with a Mr. Paxton, the department chairman, who seems both suspicious of Molly Marks and attracted to her, an old friend of Sandra Shearer's, class of '68?—really? but isn't Molly much younger?—and Molly blushes prettily and says, "Oh I'm not as young as I look." Mr. Paxton doesn't remember Sandra Shearer and is more honest about it—"My capacity to remember Sandys has eroded dramatically over the past twenty-five years"—but he does remember the McEwan twins, "Ah yes—James and Jonathan," as he says unhesitatingly, with a look not unlike Mr. Muller's. He tells Molly that it was he who made Jonathan, the more tractable of the two, wear an identification bracelet—a large, easily visible one—so that people could tell the twins apart; but of course James, the prankster—"Really a quite brilliant boy, but sometimes a bit demonic: I've often wondered what became of him"—then began to wear one too.

"Jonathan was one of my best students at the time," Mr. Paxton says, "but, like many twins—halves, I should say, of a set of twins—he was difficult to get to know well. He once wrote an impressionistic little piece on twins which I can remember to this day: quite uncanny, really, to the effect that he felt both more secure in the world physically, because 'he' was duplicated, yet less secure in other ways, than other peo-

ple, 'normal' people, because everything he did or even considered doing was anticipated by his twin, whom he thought
of, I believe, as older. Older by ten minutes—!''

"Eleven," says Molly.

Mr. Paxton looks at Molly quizzically. "Are you an old
friend of the McEwan boys too?''

Molly laughs, says lightly, "As you said—it's difficult to
get to know twins well.''

Molly next speaks with a Mrs. Flynn, a Miss Kizer, a Miss
Hennecott, older members of the faculty who try their best
to recall Sandra Shearer '68, a good girl an attractive girl
active and popular and wasn't she a class officer and didn't
she graduate with honors and—here Miss Hennecott, the
girls' physical education teacher, pauses and strokes her temple, her warm brown eyes looking pained—didn't she have
some sort of misfortune after leaving Wellcome, some years
later, ''—A younger sister of hers was a student here too and
I seem to remember her telling me that Sandra had had some
kind of accident, was hospitalized for a long time—'' and her
voice trails off into silence and Molly Marks leans forward
sharply, "Accident? What kind of an accident?'' and the
woman, still stroking her temple, says, frowning, "I don't
believe it was a traffic accident, I seem to recall it had something to do with . . . sports?—sports of some kind? hunting,
or sailing, or—no now I'm thinking of another student, another Sandy, some years later, who drowned in a speedboat
accident—Please excuse me, my memory is rather vague,''
she says, ''—and this happened some years ago.''

Then there's portly perspiring Mr. Bassett, teacher of math,
who seems rather lonely in his office, and more than willing
to talk with Molly Marks, though he has to confess he doesn't
remember much—indeed, anything—about Sandra Shearer.
"She may not have been an outstanding student in my subject," he says apologetically. He does remember the Mc-
Ewans, of course—James and Jonathan: who could fail to
remember them?—they were something of a novelty at the
school for the four years they were here, not just twins but
identical twins and not just identical twins but—and here he
pauses, frowning, blinking, searching for the right words—

somehow *more* than, *more intense* than, even "identical" twins.

Both boys were excellent students in math though math wasn't their primary subject. They earned high grades, virtually always identical grades, but it was uncanny, Mr. Bassett says, the way they would come up with identical answers on tests even when one of them might have worked out a problem incorrectly, making a small error in the proof. Nonetheless he'd supply the right answer: no word for it but *uncanny.* "When other students do that sort of thing you know immediately they've cheated, but I monitored James and Jonathan carefully and they never cheated, I'd swear to that."

Molly says it sounds as if they were reading each other's mind and Mr. Bassett says no, not exactly, one was reading the other's mind but the other was merely being read. "James was the more active of the two, Jonathan the more passive—if I remember correctly," he says. "James was both like and unlike Jonathan, depending upon his mood. When he chose he mimicked Jonathan so that Jonathan's attempts to distinguish himself from James were futile—it was an ongoing prank of James's, and perhaps it *was* funny. It was certainly unnerving to be around them and not to know which was which. Or if you were speaking with one of them you'd have to take it on faith that the boy was who he claimed to be because sometimes James impersonated Jonathan and sometimes he gave the deliberate impression of 'impersonating' himself—as if he were his twin! Though Jonathan would never impersonate James, so far as anyone knew." Mr. Bassett pauses, smiling. He seems to take it for granted that Molly is as fascinated with his remarks as he is. "In any case we all felt genuine relief when they graduated. No one objected in the slightest when our headmaster made an unofficial ruling, post-1968: *no more twins at Wellcome.*"

There are three listings for *Shearer* in the telephone directory for Fitchburg, Massachusetts, none of them *Sandra Shearer.* Molly takes down the numbers the long distance operator gives her but hesitates to call. What will she say if she does contact "Sandy"? How can she present herself?

Easier in a way for her to drive to Fitchburg and determine which Shearer is which and simply go ring the doorbell. . . . "Hello, you don't know me, my name is Molly Marks and": and what?

Another day, perhaps. Molly is feeling tired suddenly. Quite exhausted, suddenly.

She does telephone Mt. Holyoke College, however. The Alumni Affairs Office tells her that Sandra Shearer graduated from the college *magna cum laude* in 1972 but is not active in the alumni association and the most recent address they have for her is Fitchburg, Mass. Molly asks for and is given the names of Sandra Shearer's roommates . . . thinking that she might, sometime, contact them, if she can't locate Sandy herself. By the time she hangs up she is feeling extraordinarily exhausted, however. As if she has been on the trail of the mysterious Sandra Shearer for a very long time.

31

Jonathan embraces Molly so hard she winces with pain.

"I've missed you."

"I've missed *you.*"

"I love you."

"I love *you.*"

Jonathan has been gone for nearly two weeks and when Molly sees him she forgets in an instant the many doubts, questions, accusations she's harbored in his absence—simply goes to him and kisses him and bursts into tears as she'd known she would. It's that simple, Molly thinks. It's all that matters.

Jonathan, his voice quavering, begs her not to cry.

"I'm home now," he says. "I won't go away again."

Molly notes that he has lost weight, just perceptibly. His face is thinner, the fine white near-invisible creases and tucks in his skin are more pronounced. And the whites of his eyes are, oddly, more pronounced. His skin has darkened from the Arizona sun, a rich olive-tan; he seems to give off heat, still. When she closes her arms around him she feels the dampness on his back as if he has sweated through two layers of clothing.

"Next time," Molly says recklessly, "—I'm going with you."

Jonathan is in the shower when the telephone rings. Molly, in the kitchen, just starting to prepare dinner, picks up the receiver in a transport of good feeling. "Hello!"

And the voice, Jonathan's, comes, eerily: "Hello Molly?"

And Molly gives a shriek and drops the receiver.

146

And Molly doesn't touch it as it bounces and swings at the end of the cord though she can hear, clearly, the voice, Jonathan's hurt baffled frightened voice *Molly? Molly what's wrong? Molly it's Jonathan what's wrong? Molly*—a miniature voice, like something in a bad but entirely convincing dream.

When Jonathan appears, hair combed damply back from his forehead, jaws freshly shaved, Molly has most of the ingredients for their meal set out neatly on the counter. Two filleted brook trout, four small red-skin potatoes, carrots, broccoli, onions, quartered lemons, fresh dill and parsley and ground thyme. She has replaced the telephone receiver; she seems to know the telephone won't ring again.

"Do you want me to help you, Molly?" Jonathan asks happily.

"Of course," says Molly. "Scrape the carrots."

That night, making love, "I've missed you," one says, and "I've missed *you*," whispers the other. Molly shuts her eyes tight and does not see the graduation photo of pretty Sandra Shearer nor does she hear Miss Hennecott's groping voice, or Mr. Bassett's strangely rhapsodic voice, she hears nothing but Jonathan's quick panting breath, and her own. So happy, thinks Molly. Nothing else, thinks Molly. Oh yes.

32 Next day Jonathan isn't quite so exuberant. Appears subdued, depressed. Molly asks him what is wrong and he doesn't seem to hear. Molly says, kissing his forehead, "Why don't you tell me about it, Jonathan?—your father, and the rest."

Jonathan takes her hand and absentmindedly kisses it. His lips feel cold, like rubber lips. But he rouses himself and says, laughing thinly, "Well—you know what they say: no one wants to hear about death unless it can be made amusing."

33 Molly Marks sipping coffee at a counter and trying to read a newspaper trying not to hear a conversation close by, a woman's lowered but perfectly audible voice: ". . . and this cyst they removed from her ovaries, fortunately it wasn't malignant but it contained the strangest most repulsive things: *hair, fingernails, and teeth.* Yes, even teeth, in that part of her body! Her doctor told her it was a 'teratoma' tumor and it was to have been her twin . . . her twin, in her mother's womb . . . can you imagine? . . . poor Connie was just devastated. He told her that something went wrong after the fertilized egg had split and the other fetus, the twin fetus, failed to develop so it was absorbed into *her* body. Can you imagine? *Can* you?''

34 In December Jonathan McEwan gives a paper ("Strategies of Self-Narratizing: A Theory") at the annual American Association of Psychotherapy conference in Washington, D.C., which is very well received, and Molly Marks, sitting in the audience, joins happily in the applause. And afterward at a crowded reception she happens to see an attractive woman in her sixties with stark white hair braided in coils around her head—the very style in which Molly Marks had considered wearing *her* hair that day. The woman is, Molly thinks, the very model of an older professional woman: a minimum of makeup, excellent posture, poise; elegantly dressed in what appears to be a Chanel suit. She is being addressed by one of the conference chairmen while several other men look on—clearly a person of some distinction, Molly thinks, admiring. How lovely to be *her!* The woman bears little resemblance to Molly's deceased mother but Molly thinks of her mother, watching her. A certain habit of lowering her eyes as she speaks, a certain quick smile that deepens into a really quite dazzling smile. . . . Molly Marks stares, hardly caring if the woman notices her. (She doesn't.) After a moment she tugs at Jonathan's arm and asks, "Who *is* that woman?" and Jonathan says ironically, "That woman? That's Agnes Wexler. Would you like to be introduced to her?"

35 And now—can she confess?

A stumbling faltering tearful dramatic monologue of having made an error, having been seduced, having lied to him, having hated lying to him, having hated herself for lying to him since he is the man whom she loves, and loves without ambiguity, doubt, hesitation— O yes.

But no: she cannot confess.

Simply cannot choke up the words.

So, numbed, she weakly and defensively and rather stupidly tries to construct yet another lie, a more elaborate lie, atop the original fairly straightforward lie.

Tells him—and he makes a show, gentleman that he is, of listening, believing—that, yes, she lied to him. Last year. Told him she was going to Agnes Wexler when she'd been going instead to a therapist of whom, she suspected, he wouldn't approve.

Wouldn't approve?—Jonathan is drawn into asking.

Yes says Molly improvising desperately (and a little drunkenly—they've both in fact been drinking, in their hotel room in Washington) because, because—

"Because—"

Molly is sitting on the edge of a ludicrously king-sized bed. A bed large enough for three—four, five?—sleepers. For three, at least.

Jonathan waits for her to continue. Since that terrible moment downstairs at the reception his manner has been inscrutable, guarded. He speaks, when he speaks, in a carefully neutral voice; he has not looked at Molly directly. He carries

151

himself with what Molly would define as a certain graceful irony—dignity—like a badly wounded creature desperate not to betray his hurt.

"Because—"

"Yes?"

"—I didn't think you would approve."

It is a feeble statement—so feeble, Molly Marks blushes with shame and frustration, to have made it! Yet, sitting there, benumbed, mesmerized, a faint roaring in her ears and a sensation of dread hilarity imminent—the hilarity one might feel watching one's life's possessions blaze up in flame, or swept away into a giant drain—she simply cannot think of anything else. If Jonathan McEwan would feed her lines, like a stage prompter—

But he only says coldly, "Yes and why did you imagine I would not approve?—to whom in fact were you going?"

And Molly, wondering why she hasn't yet broken down, dissolved into tears, shakes her head mutely.

Don't know?—or can't say?

The telephone rings. Jonathan answers it. His tone changes immediately, he's friendly, warm, an old classmate, friend, yes he'd like very much to have a drink with him and his wife, yes certainly, how about later that afternoon?—no, in fact, how about now?

Back in Lindesfarne Molly hears herself say, again falteringly, feebly, "I think I began lying to you because I wanted to please you. . . . I'd tried to be accepted as a patient of Dr. Wexler's but she couldn't take me on, it was nothing personal just that she had all the clients she could handle and I would have had to wait and I, I . . . I'm so embarrassed! ashamed! . . . I did this stupid impulsive thing I knew you wouldn't approve of because I was hurt, or angry, or . . . self-destructive. Jonathan, I contacted a therapist out of the Yellow Pages. *Out of the Yellow Pages.*"

Jonathan looks at her now, stares at her, now—with a look of shocked pity. "Molly—out of the Yellow Pages?"

"I—I don't know why I did it," she says with a child's instinctive puzzlement shading into (yes! at this moment of all moments!) stubborn self-defensiveness, "—except that it had something to do with resenting her, and resenting you. And the woman I did go to, for a while, she wasn't, really, all that bad . . . just not first-rate. Not on Dr. Wexler's level, or yours."

A feeble attempt to flatter, here. But Jonathan is too distracted to notice.

". . . She was a perfectly nice woman about your age and her office was in Manhattan, on the Upper West Side, and I . . . I did get something, I'm sure I got something, out of my sessions with her. . . . I *liked* her as a person," Molly says, vaguely, desperately, not daring to look at Jonathan's face for fear she will see that of course he doesn't believe her, why in God's name should he believe her?—stumbling and faltering and improvising her disingenuous lie. ". . . and eventually I felt sorry for her and didn't want to break off seeing her until finally, finally . . . I did."

For a long terrible moment Jonathan says nothing. He continues to regard Molly with his look of pity, regret, subtle contempt.

"I see," he says. "And when did all this take place?"

"When? I, I don't remember the exact dates—"

"And then you began taking a class at Columbia, with—what was his name?—or have you forgotten? And naturally you had to stay overnight in Manhattan."

"Well—it seemed convenient."

"Yes. I'm sure it was convenient."

Jonathan speaks lightly and ironically, without anger.

"I'm sure you enjoyed yourself, and, as you say, you did get something out of it . . . your anonymous therapist, and your seminar at Columbia."

"She isn't anonymous, her name is, was, I mean is," Molly says desperately. "—Shearer."

"Shearer?"

Molly has not meant to say this name of course. Yet it has leapt, unbidden, to her tongue.

"Shirer," she says, her heart beating rapidly, "S-H-I-R-E-R."

"Shirer," Jonathan repeats.

Again, a terrible silence.

"Her first name is just initials," Molly says, still quite desperate, "—I've forgotten what they are exactly. I mean, that's how she was listed. I never—"

"Shirer," Jonathan says slowly. "Not Shearer."

"Yes."

Jonathan turns away. (It is an awkward rushed time, he is due to leave the apartment in a few minutes and Molly, not yet dressed, her hair not right and her face not right, is due to leave in another half-hour but cannot bring herself to think that far ahead: just standing here trembling, pale, appealing.) Jonathan sighs, and says, " 'Shirer.' A woman. On the Upper West Side."

Molly says defensively, "Well—she may have moved her office. She may have left Manhattan altogether."

"Yes," says Jonathan, going for his coat, glancing at Molly with an ironic smile, "—yes, there's always that possibility."

Hardly an hour later, at the Foundation, there is a telephone call for Molly Marks from Jonathan McEwan. Will she take the call? Molly's young secretary asks. And Molly has no choice but to say yes.

At first, hearing the voice, she thinks it might be James's and not Jonathan's. But of course it is Jonathan: "I think we should separate, Molly. Temporarily."

Molly begins to cry.

"—Molly please don't. Please, please don't. This is hard on us both, but—" There's a moment's silence as if Jonathan too is about to cry. Then he says, not unkindly, "It's just that I love you and I can't trust you. I love you—and I can't trust you. That's it," Jonathan says, "—and that's everything."

Molly, crying, is too distraught to think, *But I can't trust you either.*

"I'll be the one to move out, of course. I'll just take a few things—unless you'd like me to take more."

Molly says in a hoarse plaintive whisper, "Jonathan, I love you—this is a terrible mistake—"

"I love you but I can't trust you," Jonathan says. *"That's* the mistake."

"But I— Please—"

"We'll talk about it tonight. Goodbye."

"You can't hang up!"

"Molly, this is an impossible time for us both. I hated to disturb you at work—and I have my own work to get to. We'll talk about it tonight when we have more time, and we're both a little calmer."

"No. Please. Let's meet right now—we can talk about it right now."

Molly is sobbing, pleading, desperate. She will despise herself afterward but cannot help herself, now.

"Don't be so upset, Molly—it will be just a temporary separation. I mean, I think of it in those terms. It will be good for us both, cleansing, therapeutic—"

"I'll take the morning off, we can talk about it now. I'll drive over to—"

"*I* can't take the morning off," Jonathan says, "—and I don't want to. Goodbye."

But that day, when Molly returns home, it is to discover that Jonathan has already moved out. And that he has taken more than simply a few things—his closet is cleared, his bureau drawers, desk, a good number of his books are missing from the shelves and the boxes containing his personal papers, documents, files et al. The glass tank, turtleless for months, is gone too.

Molly pours herself a glass of bourbon and swallows down the first mouthful without flinching. A plain white envelope addressed to Molly lies on the dining room table and she is in no hurry to open it. Why not celebrate, to a degree?—after all she has gotten through what was the first day, without her knowing, of the "temporary separation."

36 *Temporary,* thinks Molly, —*separation.*

Testing the words, weighing them. As if, in her numbed state, she really doesn't know what they mean: how they connect. Or how, light as they are, mere words, mere air, they have the power to give such pain.

37

"But why, except to hurt me?"

"Why not? A bit? As you'd hurt me."

"*I!*—hurt *you!*"

"Of course, Molly dear. Don't be disingenuous, even over the phone. Surely you knew I'd grown inordinately fond of you."

Molly feels a moment's stab of pleasure. She knows how enormously difficult it is for James McEwan to utter those words.

But she says bitterly, "You *did* hurt me. That last time, in your apartment—"

"Are you still moping over that?"

"You raped me—I could have reported you to the police."

" 'Rape' is an extravagant charge, Molly," James says carefully. "I had not considered you a hysterically inclined woman, apart from this."

"You son of a bitch—"

"Why persist in imagining you've been raped when in fact you were merely passively involved in a certain sexual act, or acts?—one might debate the issue of which of us was, in truth, 'raped' in the most profound sense of the word. Surely the truth is less abrasive to your pride?"

"I don't believe this. I'm not going to listen to this."

"Nietzsche has an aphorism: 'I did this,' says memory. 'I cannot have done this,' says pride. Eventually, memory yields."

"Fuck Nietzsche."

"Not a good idea, dear—the man was a curious combination: both morbidly chaste, and syphilitic."

157

* * *

"—But you did hurt me, and I'm not going to give you the chance to hurt me again," Molly says. "Next day I lost the baby."

"Lost the baby?"

"After what you did. After—all that. Next morning I started bleeding heavily, I had a miscarriage—"

"You never told me that."

"Why should I have told you! I despise you—I don't intend to see you again."

"But you were scarcely pregnant, as I recall. Still waiting to hear the results of the laboratory test. You could not have had a 'miscarriage,' surely—"

"God damn you, I bled—I bled a lot. I was practically hemorrhaging—"

"Molly, you lost tissue, not a fetus. Nothing approaching a 'baby,' so early in your term. Don't be extravagant."

"What do you know, you—"

"And how did Jonathan take this?"

"He didn't exactly know."

"Didn't know you were 'practically hemorrhaging'?"

"Didn't know I had been pregnant."

"Because you didn't want him to know."

"Because—"

"Because you didn't want him to know."

"And all this, I see, is on my head," James says, mock-mournfully. "Because I'd made the error of falling—a bit—in love with you."

Molly laughs. She is lying in a tangle of pillows and bedclothes, telephone receiver tucked under her chin. Cigarette in one hand and a glass of bourbon in another. The word *love* is obscene-sounding in James McEwan's voice but it interests her nonetheless.

"If I had really wanted to hurt you I might have told Jonathan about you, about us, when we were together in Arizona," James says. "But of course I didn't—I resisted."

Molly would like to ask James about the Arizona visit; what sort of relationship Jonathan has with his parents; why

Jonathan lied, or misrepresented, James's part in it. But she feels it would be a betrayal of a kind, of Jonathan—prying into his private life by way of his twin. Or would it? She asks impulsively, "How long were you there, in Arizona? Jonathan stayed almost two weeks."

"I was there for the funeral, mainly," James says carelessly.

"You *were* there?"

"Of course. Why do you ask?"

"Jonathan said—"

"Jonathan said—?"

Molly stops short. She *is* betraying Jonathan.

"Did he talk to you about me? Really?" James asks almost eagerly. "I thought the self-righteous little prick refused to acknowledge my existence."

"He doesn't talk about you, really," Molly says quickly.

"But you were going to say something. What were you going to say?"

Molly closes her eyes. What is she doing? And why? She cannot shake the conviction that, when she speaks with James McEwan, when she is in James McEwan's presence, she is where she must be, where, in some mysterious sense, she belongs. Jonathan is too good for me—is that it? Or is she too good for Jonathan?

"What were you going to say, Molly?" James persists.

She says, stammering, "Just that—well—Jonathan told me you weren't at the funeral."

"Wasn't at the funeral?" James asks sharply.

"He said—I don't remember exactly what he said," she says weakly. "Except he told me you weren't there. That you didn't take 'family' seriously."

Molly realizes that she is hoping James will corroborate Jonathan's story: will assure her that, no, of course not, *her* lover would not lie to her.

Instead, James sounds vaguely hurt. "I don't suppose I take 'family' as seriously as he does, but— But still, I *was* there. And he said I wasn't?"

"I really don't remember what he said," Molly says. "Maybe he didn't say that at all."

"I thought Jonathan never talked about me."

"Oh, he doesn't."

"Then what is this all about?" James asks ironically.

Molly says, faltering, "I was wondering if—"

"If I *was* there, as I say I was, or if I *wasn't*, as Jonathan claims?"

So succinctly, and so irrefutably, put. Molly rubs the back of her hand against her forehead. One of them is lying and she doesn't want to know, does she, which. Doesn't want to know.

James says defensively, "I flew out. Of course. Couldn't avoid it—he was my father, after all. Not that he knew me, or Jonathan for that matter—we were always too clever. So Jonathan says I skipped the funeral? I wonder why." He pauses. Molly can hear him breathing close against the phone. "Probably because *he* would have liked to skip the funeral and didn't dare."

"I don't think so," Molly says. "I don't think that was it."

"Family life doesn't interest me, it's true," James says with more of his usual arrogance. "Except, perhaps, as anthropological material."

"Yes, Jonathan has told me you weren't close to any of your relatives."

"Has he! Odd he should say anything about me at all."

"*Were* you ever close?"

"No," says James, annoyed. Then, "Only as a child. One can hardly help what one does, as a child."

"And Jonathan—?"

"Jonathan is dutiful, Jonathan is 'good.' Or 'good-seeming.' As a child he would have been a thoroughly ordinary, normal, altogether conventional child, were it not for me. He tries, I suppose," James says, laughing harshly, "—to compensate for *me.*"

"Did you get along as children?"

"We did, and we didn't—like any other children." James's tone has shifted; reminds Molly of Jonathan's—subtly evasive, resentful. "Ask Jonathan if you're curious about our childhood; not me. It's rather posthumous, to *me.*"

Molly tells James about the incident in Washington, and James begins to laugh before she has even finished; and, touched suddenly by a sense of her own absurdity, Molly begins laughing too—hoarse mirthless sounds that resemble choking. Tears run down her cheeks. "What sort of expression had he on his face when you asked who Wexler was?—poor Jonathan!" James says.

"Why think of *him?*—I'm the one who's suffering."

"He *has* moved out?"

Molly sips her drink. "It's a temporary separation."

"And all because he'd caught you in a lie?"

"Because—I don't know why."

"Perhaps it was the crudeness, the awkwardness, of the lie," James says cheerfully. "Though my brother has a professional reputation for being pious and 'ethical' he is also, I suspect, as much of an aesthete as I."

"He says I violated his trust and from now on he won't be able to believe me. And he's right—I did violate his trust."

And I am violating it now, Molly thinks. Splashing another inch of bourbon into her glass.

Stretching and sighing and flexing her bare, wriggly toes.

James says, "So you told him you were going to another therapist?—not me, of course."

"I made up a name. Out of the blue."

"Poor Molly-Holly. Poor hapless girl. Was it a believable name?"

"Shirer."

"What?"

"S-H-I-R-E-R."

James says nothing for so long that Molly wonders if he has set the receiver down. Then he says, "That must have given him pause."

"No it didn't," Molly says quickly.

"Well, in any case, I suppose he believes you—wants to believe you. He would have believed anything poor Sandra told him except, out of pigheadedness, she— But that, of course, is her; not you. *You* are much more skilled in the ways of the world."

"What about her? Sandra? 'Pigheadedness'—what do you mean?"

"Ask him."

"You know I can't ask him."

"You'd marry him, have a baby with him, but not ask him a simple question or two?"

Molly backtracks. Molly says, "You think he *might* believe me, then. No matter how clumsily I lied."

"If he loves you, he'll believe you. Eventually. Love always precludes, or excludes, truth. Haven't you noticed? It makes truth irrelevant."

"But it will always be between us. All this."

"Yes," says James, drawing a luxuriant breath. "It will always be between us."

"I mean—between Jonathan and me."

"No, dear Molly—between Jonathan and you and me. *That* is the definition of 'us.' "

They talk another time. Cozily, recklessly. A bit drunkenly. "You really love me, Molly, and not Jonathan," James says, teasing. "Don't you?"

"Fuck you," says Molly.

"Don't you."

"Since Jonathan is absent, James must now be welcome. I could get in my car and be at your door, dear Molly, by eleven P.M. And in your bed. And—"

Molly shudders. "No. That's enough."

"Don't you remember our lovely times? They *were* lovely, weren't they?"

"No."

"Shall I drop by tomorrow, a bit earlier? Seven thirty, say? Jonathan being absent . . ."

Molly hears, or imagines she hears, a key in the lock. Her heart pounds violently.

". . . and we'll resume. Where we left off."

Molly listens. Hears nothing further. But she is frightened; chastised. She must hang up. "If you come out here I won't open the door. *Don't* even think of it."

"Of course you'll open the door," James says sharply.

"You miss me as much as you miss Jonathan. You miss me *more*—considering that I contain Jonathan."

"You're crazy."

"You don't for an instant believe that, you silly little twat."

These words drive Molly wild—she begins screaming, sobbing, "I hate you—it's all your fault—you bastard—fucker—*devil!* You are the *devil!*"

She slams the receiver back into its cradle so hard it falls out onto the bedside table, and onto the floor, pulling the telephone down with it. She lies there trembling listening to the quick percussive beep-beep-beep that is the very sound of madness.

38 When she unlocks the door to the apartment, steps cautiously inside, sets her briefcase and packages down . . . her heart trips absurdly with hope: Jonathan might be here.

Of course he isn't, and he won't be. But he *might* be, by the rules of logic. So her heart trips, absurdly, with hope.

"Jonathan . . . ?"

Silence. A faintly mocking jeering silence.

The days have become a week, the week nearly two weeks . . . and Jonathan does not return. He is staying at a Holiday Inn within walking distance of his office; Molly remains in the apartment which she has come to dread. (Which begins to exclude her: its emptiness violated when she enters it, its solitude defiled. A habitation designed for *two-as-one* and not *one* and what right has she here?)

Jonathan, as the offended party, has asked Molly not to contact him. Not at his office of course (Dr. McEwan has always been fastidious about "unprofessional" interruptions) and not at the Holiday Inn (to her embarrassment Molly has in fact tried to call Jonathan there—was told by the switchboard operator that no calls were to be put through to that room but would she like to leave a message?). Jonathan telephones Molly every day, however, without fail, in the early evening: asks how she is and speaks briefly of himself and listens, seemingly sympathetically, to what she has to say.

Am I on trial? Molly wonders.

She is made to recall Jonathan's paper on "strategies of narratizing"; his theory that human beings impose a more or less

164

arbitrary narrative framework upon their more or less formless lives in order to tell their lives to themselves and others, presenting their actions in the best possible light—usually as heroes but sometimes, surprisingly, as victims. "Innocent" victims. Molly wonders if she is a victim, innocent or otherwise; if that isn't, in a way, the story of her life. "If you are a victim, how do you become a hero?—heroine?" she once asked Jonathan. Jonathan looked at her smiling as if she'd said something witty he hadn't quite got. "I was describing, in my paper, the way people 'tell' stories about themselves," Jonathan said. "Truth isn't an issue—simply the phenomenon of narrative."

"Truth is irrelevant, then?"

"Truth is not irrelevant but it isn't an issue in this theory."

"But if you are a victim how *do* you become a hero?" Molly persisted.

Jonathan threw up his hands; laughed; said, "—Try doing heroic things, maybe."

Now Molly considers herself admirable if she merely gets through the day without breaking down. Without exposing her shakiness, her grief, to others—to her co-workers at the Foundation, to acquaintances like Jenny. In their eyes Molly Marks has always seemed stylish, enviable, "superior" in some indefinable but incontestable way: now she must (mustn't she?) keep up the performance. She wonders if Jonathan is right—if life is really formless, its apparent structure only apparent, everyone involved in degrees of frenzied storytelling, fabricating, lying—and to what end? "—All I know is, I love you," Molly tells Jonathan quietly. "And I don't want to live without you."

Thinking, is this true? Don't want to live, or won't be able to live?

Jonathan shifts uncomfortably and says, as if they'd been debating the issue for a long, long time, "—But you were unfaithful to me."

"I wasn't. It wasn't—that simple."

She begins to cry. Jonathan will not touch her. He says, stiffly, drawing just perceptibly back, "I wish I could believe you, Molly. Because I certainly love you."

* * *

As if sensing in Molly Marks some secret hurt, some hair-line fracture of the soul that renders her not only mortal but accessible, Jenny Owen begins more conspicuously to seek Molly out—asks if she's free for coffee, if she's free for lunch, walks with Molly to Molly's car as if there were something unspoken between them Molly is slow to acknowledge. Molly, thinking ahead to the apartment, to that moment when, unlocking the door, she steels herself against its emptiness even as—the shamelessness of hope!—she thinks, He *might* be here, finds herself distracted in Jenny's presence; vaguely embarrassed; annoyed. "How is your friend, I've forgotten his name—Jonathan?" Jenny asks, standing close; and Molly says, "Fine, he's fine, yes his name *is* Jonathan."

Jenny has a lover too. Jenny has a lover named Phil—divorced, with three children; *almost* divorced, that is. A sweet guy but he's got a bad temper, Jenny tells Molly—you find that in men don't you, sweet-natured then something happens and they reveal this other side to themselves, my husband, I mean my ex-husband, *he* was the one—Molly makes an effort to listen; to actually hear. Molly makes an effort (it *is* an effort—she's not only in a raw rotten despairing mood but she has never been a very sympathetic person, at least with other women) and after a few minutes she is caught up in Jenny's predicament (Jenny's term: "predicament")—whether to continue to see Phil though she doesn't love him exactly but she's lonely and he's lonely and so forth and so on but he *does* have this mysterious bad temper and around the children that isn't such a good thing is it?

Molly says, "I wish I could help you, give you advice, but I, I—" She pauses; blinks away tears; doesn't cry but comes dangerously close—the pain and anger of grief contorting her face. "I don't know enough about him, or about you. I mean—I'm in no position to know."

"Would you like to meet Phil?" Jenny asks. She is standing close to Molly, observing her closely. "—You and Jonathan, the four of us, we could go out to dinner sometime. Or maybe—"

"Yes," says Molly, backing discreetly away, "—sometime. That's a good idea."

"I'll call you, shall I?"
"Oh yes," says Molly. "Sometime."

And another time, in her office, at her desk, one of Molly's older male colleagues suddenly begins to tell her, unbidden, wholly unexpectedly, of *his* predicament—he is forty-seven years old and has a wife (who teaches high school) and several children (oldest twenty-one, youngest sixteen) and, to his shame, to his unmitigated unqualified everlasting shame, he is making so pitiful a salary he might as well be, let's say, uneducated, no college degrees, a trucker or a dockworker, no probably in fact men with those jobs make more than he does since they're unionized—"It just gnaws at my heart," he says. Staring at Molly Marks and shaking his head slowly. "The two of us working—two professional salaries—but do you know what teachers make?—less than I do—and something unanticipated happens like my sixteen-year-old, my daughter Hilary, she has these strange pinching sensations in her back, sometimes stabbing pain so she can't walk, starts to cry, we've taken her to a neurologist for a CAT scan and they can't find the trouble so we're scheduled for a series of tests at Columbia Presbyterian and the cost of it, the cost of it, Jesus Christ it scares me silly, the cost of it beyond what the insurance will pay—it just scares me silly." He shakes his head again, fixes his mournful eyes on Molly, eyes, she thinks, rather like her own, misting over with tears. Molly fights the impulse to cry with him; hears herself say, without thinking, "—Maybe I could lend you money—"

He stares at Molly; a wave of embarrassment sweeps over him. "You're sweet, Molly, but—but, you know, I didn't come in here to ask to borrow money."

"I realize that, but—"

"I wanted, I don't know, just to talk, I guess—"

"Oh I know," Molly says, confused. "I know."

Her offer is naive, of course, and whether she actually means it (in that instant, suddenly vulnerable, she *did* mean it—though she probably hasn't more than $500 in her savings account) she realizes that nothing she could give this man would be in any way adequate to his needs.

"But thank you just the same," he says. "I'm touched.

I'm really moved. You *are* sweet.'' And after this conversation, when he and Molly meet, he stares at her with an indecipherable expression—as if there were a special connection between them, a secret of some kind, to which neither would ever allude.

39 "At least, these days, I don't care what I eat, or how much," Molly Marks says, "—I don't have to worry about putting on weight."

Jonathan winces as if Molly has said something crude. She recalls his dislike of her jokes; her brash bright defiant insouciance; she wonders if she should back down, apologize, or push head-on—why not turn everything into a joke?

They have lunch together in White Plains, in the very restaurant to which James took Molly; but the restaurant is disappointing that day, not nearly so elegant as Molly seems to recall. (As Jonathan McEwan is not nearly so adroit with the maitre d' and the waiter as James was.) And they have dinner together at Jonathan's Holiday Inn, in a massive dining room decorated, as Molly notes, in "restaurant-Mediterranean"—sinuous vines and clumps of gigantic waxen grapes, poster-murals of Italian scenes, even a very white fake-marble statue of a female, nude, with classical aspirations. "The bizarre thing is, you could come to like it here," Jonathan says. "I mean—if you had no life. Nothing but surface."

"*Is* there anything but surface?" Molly asks.

"Molly, don't. Please."

"Don't what?—I'm simply asking. Wishing. If things were just surface—" Her voice trails off. She wants to say I wouldn't be hurt, wouldn't *bleed:* but that sounds like the rankest self-pity. And no doubt it is.

As they prepare to leave Jonathan says, "You'll get over it."

And Molly, stung as if he'd slapped her, flares up angrily,
"I don't want to get over it—do you?"

Next day at 6:30 P.M., at his usual time, Jonathan telephones. And, as soon as he hangs up, the phone rings again—
it's James.

Only a coincidence, Molly tells herself. Her palms sweat-
ing.

James is in a high-spirited mood, not transparently arrogant, not too obviously threatening. Telling Molly that, if he
drives all the way to Lindesfarne, she must open the door to
him; it's only good manners.

"Considering, after all, you've opened so much more to
me in the past," he says.

Molly says through tight-clenched jaws, "If you show up
here I'll call the police."

"Will you!" James says, whistling. If he's truly surprised,
however, or incensed, he gives no sign: his good mood is
impenetrable. "Then you'll have to come into the city to see
me, one of these nights."

"Never," says Molly, hanging up.

Why not ask him point-blank about Sandra Shearer: who
was she to you, what happened to her, what did you, or your
brother, do to her. *I demand to know.*

Why not confess to him, yes I made a mistake, yes I did
something incomprehensible, will you forgive me, can you
forgive me, Oh Jonathan please—I became involved with the
very man you hate and fear most in the world *and I don't
know why.*

But simply rehearsing such scenes leaves Molly Marks
weak, short of breath. Standing in her bathroom staring at
herself in the mirror wondering why, why, why had she ever
done it—how could she have been so blithe and shallow and,
yes, self-destructive, stupidly self-destructive—dialing James
McEwan's number in the city as she had, so many months
ago; making an appointment, so casually, with his receptionist. What seems to be your problem? the woman had asked

and had not Molly responded with a jest of some kind—
fortunately, she can't remember what she said.

As if the whole matter were a joke. An episode in, say, a
movie—a romantic mystery of a kind in which, in the end,
things worked out tidily; and, of course, for the best. The
triumph of love, the defeat of hate.

As if life itself were a joke. Perhaps that was it.

And Molly Marks of so little significance, anything she
does has no significance. Perhaps that was it.

One Sunday afternoon in late January Jonathan comes to
the apartment for some books—which, with unusual care,
Molly has packed for him in three small navigable cardboard
boxes—and they have a drink, two drinks, and, to Molly's
delight, end up making love for the first time since the separation. Then, incredibly, Jonathan apologizes and prepares
to leave. Taking, of course, the books.

Molly follows him to the door, shaken, dazed. She hears
herself saying, or is she begging, "I can't live without you—
I don't want to live without you."

Jonathan's response is immediate and savage. "Don't say
such things, Molly—you know better. That's emotional
blackmail and—you know better."

He leaves; Molly slams the door behind him; then opens
it, and calls down the corridor, "—It may be emotional
blackmail but it happens to be the truth too. And you know
it."

40 And so out of despair, or rage, or loneliness—or is it spite?—Molly Marks makes a serious blunder. Refuses to allow James McEwan to visit her but, on an impulse, drives to Manhattan to visit *him.*

And it's an error, as she realizes almost immediately: she wants to see Jonathan again, not this man; not this mirror-image of Jonathan. Even the initial sight of James in his doorway, the heart-stopping trompe l'oeil of his face, head, body, is not what she anticipated.

Molly says, stammering, "I can't stay long."

James says, smiling, "You'll stay just long enough."

But it isn't right. She isn't going to make love with him, shrinks involuntarily from his touch; isn't, despite the man's charm (and this evening he *is* charming—outdoes himself), quite the Molly Marks she once was. She remembers her old audacity with astonishment, and shame. How could she have been so brazen, so ignorant—approaching this dangerous man as if, in a purely literal sense, he were only another aspect of Jonathan and not himself: a man she scarcely knows.

"What *is* the matter, Molly?" James asks in a kindly voice.

Molly hides her face and begins to cry. Though knowing how this will offend James, and how seriously it might mar her appearance—but she doesn't care. "I don't want to live," she whispers.

"Don't be absurd," James says. Indeed he is offended. He adds, in Jonathan's very tone, "That sort of thing is emo-

172

tional blackmail, surely you're sophisticated enough to know."

He takes Molly's head between his strong fingers and draws the skin back from her eyes. Molly winces. The pain yields a certain pleasure but still Molly winces. James regards her, for a moment, with Jonathan's searching scrutiny. (Is this woman suicidal? Will she involve me?—us?) Then his expression relaxes, turns comfortably cynical. "Despair is rage turned inward, Molly-Holly. *You* don't want to die, you want it that someone else dies."

Molly tries to shut her eyes but James is holding them open. She tries to wrench herself free of his grip but he holds her too tight.

"A pity, sweetheart," he says. "I rather missed you and I'd flattered myself you missed me. Even Danton missed you—didn't you, Danton?"

As James releases Molly the cat leaps atop the white piano to stare at them. His tail is unusually bristling and erect.

"Danton!" Molly says. "I love Danton." But when she goes to pet the tortoiseshell he stands perfectly immobile, stiff, not preening or arching his back. He regards her with fierce intelligent eyes that, were Molly given to such extravagant flights of fancy, would seem to penetrate her soul.

"Danton—don't you love *me?*"

James says in a kinder voice, "Let's be friends, at least. Let's go out to dinner as we'd planned. A client and her husband took me last week to this superb Northern Italian restaurant on East Sixty-sixth—"

Molly is still stroking Danton; trying to charm Danton. "Don't you love me a *little?*" she says.

Annoyed, James pulls her away. "Don't make me jealous of Danton too," he says lightly. "Let's go out to dinner as we'd planned. And—see what evolves."

Molly rubs the skin around her eyes thinking Yes? No? Does it matter? Her last conversation with Jonathan, the previous evening, was one of her bright blithe phony conversations—she'd told Jonathan not to trouble calling her this evening, she was going to be away. Jonathan asked her where and she said, "Away."

Now she laughs suddenly. She's ready for a drink.
"Why not?" she says. "Seeing that I *am* here."

"There was a game the two of us played when we were
very little, hardly more than babies," James says. "One of
us would raise his hand for no reason and the other would be
obliged to raise *his* hand. One of us would jump and the other
would have to jump. Or run—stomp across a sofa. Or yell.
Scream. Smash something. Throw a tantrum." James pauses,
smiling. It is a queer reflective smile, like a smile Molly has
sometimes seen on Jonathan's face—though not often. "We'd
get very excited—completely out of control. My poor mother
was afraid of us in these states. She had a difficult time telling
us apart and our father was really at a loss. He called us both
'Son.' "

Molly says, "I suppose you took the lead, and Jonathan
had to follow."

"No. Sometimes I took the lead and sometimes he took
the lead but most of the time it seemed simply to happen—
neither of us was in control."

Molly shivers. "That sounds rather frightening."

"Not at all," James says slowly. "It was rather nice. I
missed it, later. When we grew out of it."

"Why not tell my priggish brother you missed *him* as a
therapist—therefore you contacted me," James says. "And
since you adore him you naturally succumbed to me; were
easily seduced. That way, you'd be flattering him. And perhaps, dear Molly, it's the truth."

Molly has stopped eating, Molly really has no appetite.
Even the expensive dinner wine tastes flat. "I can't tell him
anything," she says. "I'm trapped."

"Come, come, don't be melodramatic."

"If Jonathan knew about you—"

"—about us—"

"—he would never touch me again. He would never see
me again."

A flicker of annoyance crosses James's face. But he says,
mysteriously, "I wouldn't be so sure about that."

"What do you mean?"

"Just that I wouldn't be so sure."

"Well," says Molly sadly, pushing away her wine glass, "I'm sure."

The dinner, despite the delicious food, is a failure; the evening a failure. What had she expected? And why? Molly realizes that she has changed, considerably—she simply isn't the person she once was. It would not surprise her, she thinks, if even her little rose tattoo had faded.

"Jonathan was always attracted to my girls, as I to his," James says casually. "From sixth grade on."

"Sandra Shearer, for one?"

James shrugs. "For one. But merely one."

"What did happen to her?"

"Nothing not of her volition."

"Yes—but what?"

"Ask *him. He* is the center of your universe." James gives the words a comical twist of his lips. "*He* has all the answers."

"Is she alive?"

"Go find out."

"Does Jonathan keep in touch with her?"

"I doubt it."

"Do you?"

James looks away; makes a slight shivering motion with his head—a gesture of fastidiousness, repugnance. "Certainly not," he says.

"Which of you did she love best?"

" 'Better,' I believe, is the correct usage."

"Jonathan, or you?"

"You'd have to ask her that."

"She *is* alive?"

"Assuredly."

"But you don't keep in touch?"

James picks up Molly's glass of wine and drains it. "Sandy was never my type, really—more Jonathan's."

"Goodnight, then?"

"Goodnight."

"You really don't want to come back to the apartment with me?"

"I really don't. I'm sorry."

"But don't *look* so sorry—positively contrite. These silly little miscalculations happen all the time."

Gallantly, even gaily, James hails a cab for Molly; waves a kiss at her as she is driven away. Afterward she will wonder whether the man was already imagining his revenge even as he stood at the curb smiling . . . or whether, at the time, he really did sympathize with her, and wished her well.

James had brushed her cheek with his lips, lightly and ceremonially. It will be the last time they touch and Molly will remember it the rest of her life.

41 At the Foundation Molly reads applications for grants, one of them from an upstate New York dance troupe with an interest in developing a cycle of experimental dances titled "Shiva: Eighteen Figures." *Shiva, the Hindu god, begins to dance at first slowly, then faster and faster, and yet faster, until the work of Creation is undone—and the world ends.*

"So be it," she says.

42 In February Jonathan flies to La Jolla for a week-long conference; the third day of his absence Molly receives a mysterious package in the mail, stamped *special delivery* and *special handling*. When she opens the package she nearly faints—inside a Styrofoam container decorated with glossy Valentine hearts is what appears to be an actual heart . . . prune-sized, raw, bloody, with a child's arrow stuck through it.

In James's hand on the accompanying card: *Dear Molly Marks, Danton gives you his heart herein; as I assure you, I do mine. XXXXX J. McE.*

My God, Molly thinks, when she recovers. The man is mad.

When James telephones Molly hangs up without speaking to him. She keeps the receiver off the hook . . . realizing she would rather miss a call from Jonathan than risk hearing James's voice again.

She sees, or imagines she sees, James's metallic-black BMW following her car when she leaves White Plains for home. A solitary driver, a man, following several car lengths behind her . . . his speed increasing when hers increases, decreasing when she slows down. She's terrified of driving to her apartment building and parking in the garage so she drives aimlessly, in a well-lighted area, for an hour or more. Finally pulls up in front of the police station. And sits there, smoking a cigarette, until she decides the danger, if there was any danger, is past.

He doesn't telephone, any longer. Is that good, Molly wonders, or not so good? Perhaps he doesn't care about actually talking to her, now.

Molly receives a telegram at the Foundation: *Please contact me, terrible misunderstanding imminent. Love, J. McE.* She crumples it and throws it into a wastebasket, her hands shaking.

And yet another telegram, a few days later, at home: *Insist please contact me, irrevocable rift must be avoided at all costs. Love, J. McE.* Again she throws it away. And doesn't, of course, call him.

She wonders, frightened, if James has lost his sense of humor. His cavalier manner—his casualness. Perhaps all along it was a mask, a disguise? As he'd accused his brother of wearing a disguise?

Noises in the night. Odd thuds, rustlings. Footsteps. Seven floors to the street and she's safe of course yet *is* she safe . . . perhaps he could get into her apartment somehow by way of the balcony.

Molly can't sleep. Molly is terrified. Sits cross-legged in bed in the darkened bedroom staring at the window. Should she call the police? (But what would she say?) Take refuge with another tenant in the building? (But what would she say?) By day her fears diminish but by night they wash over her leaving her exhausted, trembling. Her obsessive thoughts of James have very nearly driven out thoughts of Jonathan.

Could that have been poor Danton's heart!—*could* the madman have done such a thing!

She brings a kitchen knife into the bedroom with her. Just in case. Wishes she had a gun. Or something larger, more easily wielded—a poker, a baseball bat. Next day, she thinks, she'll buy a baseball bat at a sporting goods store, but next day, of course, her fears begin to diminish; seem rather silly. Would a man of James McEwan's position and wealth really

trouble to drive so far simply to harass her? threaten her?
Granted his pride has been hurt, is Molly Marks really so
important to him? —He'd always impressed upon her the fact
that she wasn't important at all. To his twin maybe but not
to him.

She considers sending him a telegram. *Please leave me
alone please I am sorry sorry sorry* but eventually discards
the idea. Why should *she* apologize? Why, if she is the victim?

43 Molly informs Jonathan that she is going to move out of the apartment at the end of March if he doesn't decide to move back by that time. The place is "too large" (she does not say "too lonely") without him.

"Move out?" says Jonathan, surprised. "Where?"

"Don't worry," Molly says. "Not to your place."

(Jonathan has left the Holiday Inn and is living now in a low-rental building where single rooms and efficiency apartments are available by the week. Molly has never been invited to visit Jonathan's apartment and guesses she never will be.)

Jonathan squeezes Molly's hand, quite hard, as if she were making an irrevocable decision. Yet he says, only, "Well— you should do what you think is best."

"Damn you," says Molly, drawing her hand away. "I hate you."

Her voice trembles; she stares at him defiantly.

Between the two of you, she thinks, I am being destroyed.

Jonathan speaks gently but rather coldly. "I can't be pressured into making a decision, Molly. You really will have to do what you think is best. As you know, I'm happy to—I mean, I want to—continue paying rent on the apartment, whether I live there or not. Just to know that it's there—"

"That I'm there."

"Yes. Of course. That you're there."

"Because you love me."

"Because, yes, I love you."

Molly laughs. Molly makes a gesture of weariness, capitulation—bowing her head, elbows on the table, drawing the soft skin back from her eyes with her fingertips. She knows she looks terrible, these days. Her skin pallid and blemished, bruiselike welts beneath her eyes from lack of sleep—at the Foundation some of her colleagues have expressed concern about her but Jonathan seems not to see, or to care. Perhaps it gratifies him that she is being punished.

She thinks—I want a gun. She thinks, suddenly, with the force of a revelation—I want a gun.

That night, Jonathan returns with Molly to the apartment, "their" apartment. And they make love, or make the attempt to do so. Molly is aware of Jonathan/James observing her, judging her, mocking her; Molly takes no pleasure in sex any longer but knows, or recalls, that there *is* pleasure to be taken . . . isn't there? It all seems rather crude, however, and pathetic. A sort of mammalian struggle, fleshy, sweaty, panting, labored, toward a release of nervous excitation meant to signal mutual feeling; an intimate bond. In a sense lovemaking is a kind of handshake but if the hands being shaken are fraudulent, what then? to what purpose? Molly begins crying and Jonathan says angrily, "Then why don't you tell me the truth?—damn you Molly, why don't you tell me the truth about your lover?" his voice harsh as if he too were about to cry. But Molly lies unmoving, mute, forearm across her face. She recalls how, straddling her, James struck her, systematically, dispassionately, whispering obscene names—*her* names—and using the soft edge of his hand so that the damage wouldn't show; or wouldn't show dramatically.

44

Molly Marks telephones the Lindesfarne Police Station very late one evening. "I think my life is in danger," she says.

"Yes? Who is this? Could you speak up, please?"

"I—I said, I think my life is in danger. There's a man who—"

"Is this an emergency? Where are you calling from?"

"It isn't an emergency. I mean—not right now. Not this minute."

"What is your name, please? Telephone number? —Are you a resident of Lindesfarne?"

Molly hesitates. "I—I want to know what you can do."

"You'll have to speak up, miss. I can barely hear you."

"I want to know what you can do."

"Someone has threatened you? Husband, boyfriend—?"

"Not exactly—"

"Is he there with you now? Is he on the premises?"

"No. I mean, not that I know of."

"What is the situation, then?"

"This man—there is this man who has threatened me. Sometimes he telephones me. He follows me in his car—I mean, I think it's him, following me in his car. I—"

"Do you know who he is?"

"Yes, of course I know who he is."

"Has he threatened you directly? Is he armed?"

"I—don't know. I mean—I don't know," Molly stammers. "He has said things to me but he hasn't exactly threatened

183

my life. I don't think he has a gun. I'm reasonably sure he doesn't have a gun. But—"

"You say he isn't there with you now? This isn't an emergency situation?"

"Not *now*—it's sometime in the future I'm—"

"Why are you calling the station now, miss?"

"I—I'm afraid to go to bed."

"You're afraid to—?"

"—go to bed. I mean—alone." Molly swallows hard. Wonders if she should hang up before the call is traced. (Would the call be traced?) "I mean—I'm here alone, I live alone, I'm afraid of this man breaking in my apartment, or, not that maybe, I live in a high-rise apartment, but I think he's following me sometimes, home from work, I'm afraid of the parking garage and I'm afraid of—going out alone— And the telephone, I'm afraid to leave it on the hook—"

"Would you like us to send over an officer, miss?"

"I—I don't think so. I mean, there's nothing—"

"What is your name? And where do you live?"

Molly pauses, trying to catch her breath. It all seems so absurd, doesn't it. If James were listening . . .

"How is this person related to you?"

"He isn't. There is no relationship. He—he's someone I used to go out with."

"Does he have a police record?"

"No of course not. I mean no—he isn't that sort of man. He's a professional man. A psychiatrist." Molly wonders why she has called James a psychiatrist: that isn't his title. "He— I think he's mentally unbalanced. Or pretending to be. He's jealous, he wants to frighten me, I don't know if he really wants to hurt me but he wants to frighten me. He sent me this hideous thing in the mail—this *heart.*"

"What?"

"A cat's heart. I think. Or an animal's heart—from a butcher shop, maybe." Molly can't seem to get her breath. She feels light-headed, dizzy. On the verge of inappropriate laughter. "—It was to warn me. To threaten me."

"You'll have to identify yourself, miss. Otherwise we can't help you."

"But what will you do? Can you arrest him?"

"If he threatens you directly, or causes physical harm, we can arrest him. If he forcibly enters your premises—"

"But I don't know where he is."

"Is he there, now? Do you have reason to think he's there, now, on or close by the premises?"

"I don't know where he is."

Molly gives a little scream of despairing laughter and hangs up.

She halfway expects the policeman to call her back but of course he doesn't.

45 By way of a friend of a friend of Molly Marks's from her Provincetown days she manages to acquire, not quite legally, a lady's revolver—snub-nosed, nickel and stainless steel, mother-of-pearl handle—a classic! Like something sported by Bette Davis or Barbara Stanwyck in a Hollywood movie of the 1940's.

The charming little handgun is a Smith & Wesson .22 caliber, fits snugly in the hand and is fully loaded with a round of bullets *but*—thinks Molly, bemused, frightened—it looks more like a toy than a deadly weapon. Is it to be taken seriously?

The young man who sells it to Molly (a bargain, he boasts, only $120) is lean and bearded, with Manson-bright eyes. That frank searching psychopath gaze. Deals drugs too and would she be interested?—highest quality coke, crack, bennies, Valium? Molly shakes her head emphatically. No.

"Ex-boyfriend bothering you, right?" he says sympathetically. Moving closer to Molly, his breath warm and fetid. "Maybe you'd like some help dealing with him—some direct help?"

"No," says Molly Marks coolly. "I can take care of myself."

46 Sandra Shearer cannot be more than eight years older than Molly Marks but—dear God—she looks like an aged, wizened woman: recessed eyes, small and unseeing; a deathly white-puckered skin, like something left too long in the water; tremors in both hands. Her body, beneath the wool-and-satin quilt, is hunched, crushed, as if broken-backed. Her arms and legs are like sticks—like a Holocaust survivor. "Oh," says Molly, shocked, faint, grasping at Mrs. Shearer's arm to steady herself, "I didn't realize—"

"That's all right, dear," Mrs. Shearer whispers. "It isn't nearly what you think."

It isn't?

Mrs. Shearer is a heavyset friendly woman, clearly a lonely woman, a desperately lonely woman, widowed and living alone with her incapacitated daughter in an attractive if rather run-down colonial house in an older residential neighborhood of Fitchburg, Massachusetts. Molly had expected the woman to be suspicious of her, doubtful of her intentions in visiting Sandra, but, to the contrary, she'd spoken warmly to Molly on the phone; saw no reason for her not to drive up the next day to visit. (Molly Marks has presented herself as an old classmate of Sandra's from Mt. Holyoke—"though probably Sandy won't remember me, after so long." Exactly why Molly wants to see Sandra after so many years of being out of contact isn't clear, but doesn't seem to be an issue.) Over the phone Mrs. Shearer explained that, though Sandra doesn't get outside much, she

does enjoy company—to a degree. Molly asked why Sandra
didn't get outside much and Mrs. Shearer said frankly,
"Well—it's her condition, Miss Marks. Or may I call you
Molly? You know about her condition, I assume, since the
accident? But she'd love to see you, I'm sure."

Which turns out not to be the case. The crippled woman
in the bed makes no effort to "see" Molly Marks at all.

As in one of her bad dreams Molly finds herself escorted
into an airless, overheated bedroom, a girl's room of sorts,
blinds drawn against the snow-bright March sunshine. But
the girl has the face of a prematurely elderly woman and the
flaccid muscle tone of an invalid. Her eyes are a cobwebby
color, the gaze unfocused, though there is a television set
near the foot of her bed, garishly colored images flickering
silently on the screen. "Sandra, say hello," Mrs. Shearer
urges. "This is an old classmate of yours from Holyoke—
Molly Marks."

"Hello Sandra," Molly says hoarsely. Though she is reel-
ing with shock and pity—and revulsion—she manages to smile
her flashy coed smile and even to extend her hand, as if
Sandra Shearer might be inclined to take it. "You probably
don't remember me, but . . ."

"Molly Marks, her name is, Sandra," Mrs. Shearer says,
as if speaking to a recalcitrant child. "Don't be rude, dear.
Look over here."

But Sandra Shearer, lying in her freshly laundered bedclothes, merely glances toward Molly with a look of frowning incomprehension—as if Molly were no more than a
flickering image in her vision, a moment's fleeting curiosity.
Her face has the look of a mask carelessly imprinted upon a
human face.

My nightmare, Molly Marks thinks. Here.

Mrs. Shearer is saying, apologetically, "Sandra *was* excited about seeing you, really; I'm sure she was. She didn't
at all mind my shampooing her hair and trying to set it. And
that pretty robe—that's her favorite. But then, suddenly, an
hour ago . . . her mood shifted."

"I'm sorry," Molly says, staring.

"She has good days and bad days and they can't be predicted,'' Mrs. Shearer says matter-of-factly. She bends over her daughter's hunched form, touches her hair in a familiar, fond gesture. ''Sandra, it's Molly Marks. From Holyoke. She's dropped by for a visit—isn't that thoughtful of her? Says she just wanted to see you, says she missed you—isn't that nice?''

But Sandra Shearer, utterly silent, doesn't seem to hear her mother. Or, hearing, doesn't care. Her eyes, vague and wandering, have drifted back in the direction of the television screen where an afternoon game show is in progress.

Molly says quietly, ''I shouldn't have disturbed her— I didn't know.''

''No, not at all, dear. You haven't disturbed us at all. We have so few visitors, these days.''

Molly sees, close up, that the afflicted woman is even more emaciated than she appeared at first—she must weigh no more than ninety pounds. Though Mrs. Shearer has outfitted her in a yellow quilted robe her bones jut nonetheless. Her forehead is whitely puckered, the bony ridges of her skull prominent. How long has she been in this ghastly condition, Molly wonders. For the past ten years? For as long as Jonathan and James McEwan have been estranged?

Sandra Shearer's hair is gunmetal-gray, and thin as an infant's. Her mother has combed it back gently from her face and fastened it with gleaming gold barrettes of the kind Molly Marks wore in junior high school.

The visit with Sandra does not last beyond five very slow very painful minutes. Molly thinks, I have met my twin.

''. . . I realize this is a bit of a disappointment to you, and a shock,'' Mrs. Shearer says apologetically, leading Molly away. ''But as I said, my daughter has good days and bad days and the doctor himself says her moods are 'idiopathic.' Do you know what that means?''

Molly guesses. ''Unpredictable?''

''Yes. Unpredictable.''

''. . . they said 'self-inflicted' but I was never convinced. It seems to me she was probably just emotional, and feeling so upset, you know, about the engagement being broken, and her fiancé refusing to speak with her, she might have been just threatening to hurt herself . . . but not to *kill* herself. Not that. She was always a religious girl. . . . She would never have knowingly done harm to herself or to any other person. It's just that she was upset, emotional, she wanted to get his attention, I think . . . desperate to get him to love her again. Because he broke it off so suddenly. Stopped loving her. And refused to see her again or even talk with her—just went away like he did. And stayed away where no one knew how to reach him."

"I see," Molly says. "Jonathan McEwan was her fiancé?"

"Did you know Jonathan, when he and Sandra were going together?"

"I may have met him a few times," Molly says. "Him and his brother James."

"But you didn't go to Wellcome, I gather?"

"No."

Molly wipes surreptitiously at her eyes. She dreads a sudden helpless display of tears.

Mrs. Shearer continues in a warm, eager voice: "They were all at Wellcome together, it was a wonderful school, and a wonderful time in their lives—Sandra was never so happy afterward, it seemed to me. Of course they all went to different colleges after graduation: Sandra to Mt. Holyoke, as you know, and Jonathan to Harvard, where he did extremely well. I don't remember where his brother went but it wasn't to Harvard. At Wellcome Sandra and Jonathan were sweethearts, and they continued to see each other through college—Jonathan was the only boy Sandra was ever really serious about, though she went out a good deal, and I know Jonathan loved *her*—he was a quiet, intense, very bright young man, like his twin but more serious, and more reliable, people said. He was in training to be a psychiatrist when it happened—the tragedy. The misunderstanding and what followed. He and Sandra were going to be married in June of the year he got his degree but then—it happened."

"What exactly *did* happen?" Molly asks carefully.

Mrs. Shearer passes her hand over her eyes—the nails are perfectly even, and gleam with a transparent pink polish—and says, sighing, "Well—I don't *know.* Of course I know what people said, what the authorities decided, and the doctors, but I don't know really—I mean, what Sandra meant by it. Because, afterward, after the accident, with the injury to that part of her brain, Sandra could never tell me. It's just the testimony of other people, mainly friends of Sandra's, girlfriends, saying what they knew of her mental state, her 'depression' they called it, after the engagement was broken. They said she talked about killing herself, she didn't want to live any longer, they said, without Jonathan, that kind of terrible reckless thing, and I don't doubt that the poor girl did say it—she loved him so much and it was such a shock. She had a job, and a good, promising job, at a magazine, but her whole life was him." Mrs. Shearer pauses, looking frankly at Molly. "But I don't believe my daughter meant it, really. A girl that age says things she doesn't always mean and she can even do things she doesn't always mean not knowing how permanent they are. Like, today, aren't they all starving themselves?—trying to look like fashion models, and some of them starving to death? *You* understand, don't you? Molly?"

"I think so. Yes."

"Would you like to see our photograph album—from those years?"

Mrs. Shearer, sitting close beside Molly, turns the pages of an overstuffed gilt-covered album, showing Molly a treasury of snapshots, formal photographs, yellowed news clippings, school publications and playbills—not surprisingly, Sandra Shearer belonged to the drama clubs at Wellcome and Holyoke, and took part in a number of productions. "Her finest role was Antigone—in that modernized version, I forget the playwright. She was wonderful as Ophelia too, at Wellcome, but the production as a whole wasn't outstanding—they were all so young, after all. Isn't she pretty?—this is the Ophelia costume. She picked wildflowers for her hair, fresh for every performance. *Isn't* she pretty . . . !"

More than pretty, Molly thinks, staring at the picture.

(She wonders how Jonathan McEwan, in love with, engaged to, this angelically beautiful girl, could ever have dissociated himself from her; could ever have fallen in love with Molly Marks.)

Mrs. Shearer turns the pages of the album slowly, lovingly. Here is her sweet-smiling daughter in a white graduation cap and gown; here is her daughter in a two-piece bathing suit, arms linked around the waists of her girlfriends; here is her daughter in a scarlet taffeta cocktail dress, wearing high-heeled brocaded shoes with cruelly pointed toes in the style of the day—her arm linked through Jonathan McEwan's. And how startlingly young, boyish, innocent, handsome, the eighteen-year-old Jonathan, in a tuxedo. . . . After a pause Mrs. Shearer says, "They made a perfect couple, Sandra and Jonathan—everyone said so. Didn't you feel the same way, Molly?"

"Yes," says Molly, staring at the photograph.

"Jonathan was a shy boy but Sandra could draw him out. A sweet boy, really . . . so we were shocked at the way he behaved. I suppose it was part of his shyness, withdrawing like that, not wanting to talk, or explain . . . 'still waters run deep' is the old saying and it's true. It's often true. Sandra never explained it satisfactorily to her father and me, didn't want to upset us, I suppose, and of course she was deeply hurt, and ashamed . . . she was a good girl, I mean a *good* girl the way girls were then, a virgin I mean . . . until whatever happened, happened. She told us that there had been this cruel thing Jonathan's brother James had done, whether on purpose or a trick, evidently he'd pretended to be Jonathan, and got Sandra intoxicated . . . she never drank, as far as I knew, I mean she never drank excessively, she wasn't ever like that. And so . . . something happened . . . that couldn't be undone," Mrs. Shearer says vaguely. With slow fussy fingers she tries to smooth out some of the wrinkled clippings. ". . . And Jonathan reacted so violently. So very jealous. I don't know how he knew, whether Sandra herself told him, or James; or . . . whatever. I don't, you know, *really* know everything that happened. But Jonathan refused to see Sandra again, just cut her off, cut his brother off too, and went away somewhere where no one could find him—just disappeared. (It turned out afterward he'd gone backpacking in the Adirondacks, alone. He was gone for fifteen days.) And Sandra was desperate. She was simply desperate. Quit her job, wouldn't talk to her friends, wouldn't talk to her father and me, just—went to pieces. She'd been so strong, it always seemed, a campus leader, so intelligent and reliable and responsible when it came to doing things for other people, but for herself—it was like she didn't value herself, didn't know how good and sweet and wonderful she was—just believed the things Jonathan must have said about her, whatever it was he said about her, that final time they talked. He was so angry he refused even to take the engagement ring back—he told her it was defiled. And poor Sandra—she didn't know what she was doing when she—did what she did. She was so young and at that age you can't know. You think you're going to live forever so you can throw it all recklessly away—at that age. It's some sort of playacting but then it turns out *real*. . . . But then what she did to herself was permanent and there were several operations, the doctors saved her from dying but certain parts of the brain were destroyed, they said, certain motor skills and the ability to talk, to 'reason' . . . well, you know.'' Mrs. Shearer wipes at her eyes with a tissue. "Jonathan *was* sorry afterward, he was devastated in fact, but of course it was too late.''

"Where did she get the gun?'' Molly asks.

"Well—nobody knew. Or would say. The police never found out—that was one of the terrible things about it, that my daughter, desperate as she was, obviously emotionally unbalanced, could go out and buy a gun—but I guess, from what I read in the paper, you can buy all sorts of illegal things if you have the money. Guns and ammunition and drugs. Sandra was living in Boston then and, in a city like that, you could probably buy a gun without much trouble if you tried.''

Despair is rage turned inward. You don't really want to die, you want it that someone else dies. . . .

Molly nods. Yes. True.

Mrs. Shearer says bitterly, "So he *was* sorry afterward—Jonathan McEwan. And the other one too. As if that did any good, made any difference, to Sandra, or to her family!—when it was too late."

Molly says, "Did he come visit her?—in the hospital?"

"Oh yes. Of course. And James too. Though James could only visit when Jonathan wasn't to be there—Jonathan hated him for what he'd done, never forgave him—I'm sure he *never* forgave him; and I hope so. I remember meeting James in the elevator, and thinking at first he was Jonathan—addressing him, you know, as if he was Jonathan—and this look in the young man's face—it's hard to describe—like he wanted to be Jonathan or actually was him, for just that minute—then remembered of course he wasn't, and introduced himself. Looking guilty, sickish—as well he should. My husband and I had met James once or twice before but really didn't know him, except, you know, with twins, there is the inclination to think that if you know one you already know the other. But the McEwan boys—"

"Were different."

"Were different. Completely. So people who knew them always said, and they were right." Mrs. Shearer turns to look at Molly, attempting a smile. "Did *you* know James McEwan?"

"No."

"Just Jonathan?"

"Yes—but not well."

"He used to call us, or write, but it's been years now—years. When my husband passed away seven years ago he sent a card but that was all. Not a word to Sandra. But—" Before she closes the album Mrs. Shearer shows Molly another snapshot, this of Sandra at about the age of seventeen, in a maroon bulky knit sweater and blue jeans, barefoot, smiling and squinting up at the camera. "I always thought that hair style, turned under like that, was ideal for Sandra—don't you think so? And her smile—so sweet."

"She was a beautiful girl," Molly says.

"Wasn't she—!"

47

THE MARK OF A MEDIOCRE MIND—TAKING
THINGS TOO SERIOUSLY.
—DIDEROT.

This telegram awaits Molly Marks upon her return home from Fitchburg.

Her first impulse, of course, is to tear it up. Her second, which she follows, is to tape it to her refrigerator door where she's drawn to looking at it, contemplating it, a dozen times a day.

48 When Molly Marks confronts Jonathan McEwan with the fact that she knows about Sandra Shearer—"your former fiancé"—Jonathan's initial response is one of stunned disbelief: he simply stares at her as if he cannot believe he hears what he hears.

"I drove up to Fitchburg the other day," Molly says, "—I spent an afternoon with them. With Mrs. Shearer mainly. She showed me a photograph album, she talked about you. About you and her daughter." Molly pauses. Her voice is trembling but perhaps Jonathan, taken by surprise as he is, his eyes narrowed in an expression that can only be called stricken, will not notice. "She told me about—what happened. So far as she knew what happened."

Jonathan gropes for the cigarette he has laid in an ashtray without seeming to know what he does: the cigarette rolls across the tabletop, almost falls to the floor. He says, in a voice that registers his shock, "How—was she? Sandra? You saw Sandra?"

"Mrs. Shearer told me 'it isn't nearly what it looks like,' " Molly says ironically.

Jonathan stares, as if uncomprehending. Molly has never seen him so—is it defenseless? undefended? He speaks in a lowered voice as if someone in the dining room, in this place of affable chattering strangers, might overhear: "Is she—unchanged?"

"I suppose that's what you would say. Unchanged."

They sit for a while in silence. A waitress comes by to ask if they are ready to order their dinners or would they like a second drink and Jonathan doesn't seem to hear so Molly says quickly, "Yes—we'll each have a second drink."

After a long moment Jonathan says, still in that lowered, cautious voice, "How did you know about Sandra?"

"Someone told me, Jonathan."

Jonathan, massive shoulders slightly hunched, sits without moving: his head bowed, mouth just perceptibly twitching. He is a man, Molly thinks, who is thinking—hard. One can very nearly feel the rapidity and heat—the desperation—of his thoughts. She says, quietly, "Did you think no one would ever tell me?—that I would never find out?"

Jonathan shakes his head in silence. Molly feels her eyes fill with tears of love, and of anger. "Did you think I would never find out?" she persists.

Finally he says, "—I should have told you." It is a statement made with numbed lips, oddly atonic; as much a question as a statement. "I—intended to tell you."

"Yes. You should have told me," Molly says.

Now, she thinks, steeling herself, he will ask who it was, who told her. He will ask, and what will she say?

But Jonathan simply says again, "—I should have told you."

Molly says impatiently, daringly, "And about your brother too—your 'identical twin.' You waited until we were moving into the apartment together to tell me and then of course you didn't really *tell* me." Jonathan looks up, apprehensive, slightly cringing. "I mean—you didn't tell me what had happened between you: why you hated him, why you never saw him or spoke of him—all that."

Their drinks are brought and set down before them and Jonathan continues to stare at Molly, his mouth twitching, the corners of his eyes pinched—in guilt, in apprehension, in slow-accumulating resentment. Molly can guess at the hard hot furious beating of his blood.

Molly cannot resist; "All this would have been avoided, if you'd told me."

" 'All this—'?"

"All this!" Molly says in a fierce little cry.

Jonathan doesn't know what she means, or doesn't want to

know; sits hunched over the table, shaggy head lowered, hair
disheveled as if with the very force of the blow he has absorbed. In his well-worn corduroy coat, tieless, his shirt open
at the throat, chin and jaws shadowy with an emerging black
beard, Jonathan McEwan looks like a man who is coming
unraveled; or, rather, like a wounded animal—clumsy, baffled, dangerous.

Molly says angrily, not entirely coherently, "—You forced
me to make my own discoveries. Since I loved you—I love
you. Since I'm in love with you. Since I—I feel my life
bound up with yours—somehow—I *know* it is bound up with
yours. And you—" Molly wipes savagely at her eyes. She
has rehearsed this scene, or its rudimentary outline, numerous times in the past forty-eight hours and does not intend to break down now. "—you didn't deceive me exactly
but you didn't tell the truth exactly and you forced me to
make my own discoveries—I even looked through your
things, Jonathan, when you were away in Arizona—the
boxes you kept in your closet—yes your private things, Jonathan, don't look so startled!—*of course I did.* You must have
known what I'm like, you must have known how I would be
tempted—aren't you a psychotherapist, after all!—a master of
others' minds after all!—Yes I looked through your things:
the prep school yearbook, for instance. Saw Sandra Shearer
in it. And you. And the scissored-out places where James
had been."

Jonathan puts his hands over his ears in a violent childlike
gesture. "Molly. Don't. Don't tell me these things."

"You forced me to make my own discoveries."

"Just don't. Please."

"You and Sandra Shearer. And James."

"Don't speak of *him,* for Christ's sake."

"I will if I—"

"Stop. No more."

Jonathan slams his fist down on the tabletop with such
force that the glasses rattle. Patrons in the next booth glance
over at them, suddenly silent.

Molly draws back. She has never seen Jonathan McEwan
so distraught: his eyes are brimming with tears and his face

gleams with perspiration. Two thoughts strike her simultaneously: *I love him* and *I don't know him.*

Jonathan swallows a large mouthful of his drink. Not looking at Molly, half shielding his eyes from her, he says, "I can't take this up again. Not again. Not now. Don't ask me to—now. Over and over, thousands upon thousands of times, thinking about it, blaming myself, *not* thinking about it, trying to get on with my life—no, I've gone through it; I've had it. What happened between her and my brother happened between them without reference to me, it excluded me, I accepted that and I've gone on with my life and of course I blame myself, I've always blamed myself, but it can't be helped—he *did* defile her, and she *did* betray me, and I *did* cut her off because I'd stopped loving her—there was nothing to be done: I stopped loving her, felt nothing for her except pity. At the most—pity. That's the way it was, and that's the way it is. I'm through with it all now."

"But Mrs. Shearer said he tricked her daughter. Your brother—"

"Of course he didn't 'trick' her—she'd always been attracted to him," Jonathan says, his voice rising in anger. "She was attracted to me initially because I was James's twin—*he* was the one she'd really wanted. But couldn't get until she'd got me—until Jonathan had something James could take."

"Wait. How do you—"

"How do *you* know? What business is it of yours? None of this has anything to do with you, Molly," Jonathan says, "—so I suggest you drop the subject. I never want to talk about it again."

"I don't think that's reasonable. That's—"

"You have no right to pry into my past—into my private life. No more than I have a right to pry into yours. I don't *want* to pry into yours."

"If you loved me, you—"

"I don't consider that love."

Jonathan has become increasingly angry; his face is dark with blood. Though she knows she is losing control of the situation Molly persists: "What do you consider love, then?"

"I don't know, Molly," Jonathan says. "—Only that I'm not the man for it."

Jonathan pays for their drinks and leaves. And Molly, left behind, trembling, exhausted, thinks, *So be it.*

49 "Once—once only," James McEwan says. "A long-delayed honeymoon—the two of us."

" 'The two of us'?—but why?" Molly says. Her voice is wire-tight; her jaws clenched in hatred.

"Why long-delayed, or why a honeymoon?—if the latter, because I've decided I adore you."

"But I don't adore you. I'm no longer one of your slavish clients."

"Indeed you *do,* Molly. I am as permanently imprinted in your soul as—my *semblable.*"

Molly Marks feels the weight, the disagreeable heat, of the telephone receiver against her ear. She says in as neutral a voice as possible, "I know about Sandra Shearer now, James. And I've told Jonathan."

For a moment there is absolute silence at the other end of the line. Molly thinks with bitter satisfaction—At last I have surprised the son of a bitch.

But James responds with seeming enthusiasm: "Do you! Did you! How really—remarkable! I wouldn't have expected it of you, to be frank. I wouldn't have expected you to dare make inquiries into your beloved's past."

"Yes," says Molly carefully. "And I've told him."

For some reason James seems not to hear; or chooses to ignore this. He says, "But I seriously doubt, dear, that you really know much about what happened. The mother spoke with you, I presume? Poor deluded woman—!"

201

"You seduced Sandra Shearer, out of jealousy. And told Jonathan. And Jonathan broke off the engagement."

"Not quite. You slander me, Molly. I never 'tell' on any-one—that would constitute a violation of my integrity. No, the hysterical girl told Jonathan herself—confessed to him. Some surpassingly preposterous story of having been tricked into thinking *I* was *he.* And naturally he was insulted to the very quick of his being—and revulsed, and outraged—because after all he was Jonathan, and not James: a self-righteous Philistine. It was Sandra's female masochism that inspired her to such folly—the desire, I should say the rav-ening hunger, to be hurt." James pauses; he has been speak-ing quickly. He adds, "But it *was* a pity—a sort of situation tragedy, you might say. I do acknowledge that Sandra, in those days, was a lovely girl—though no lovelier, dear Molly, than you."

"I saw her. Up in Fitchburg. In her mother's house."

"Yes. I believe you said so," James says uneasily. "And I am, as *I've* said, duly impressed."

"You don't seem curious about her—how she looks, the condition she's in? What their lives are, there in Fitchburg, day after day—?"

"I suppose you are blaming me?"

"Does that seem like an unreasonable assumption?"

"And Jonathan?"

"Yes. And Jonathan."

"But not Sandra herself?"

Molly hesitates. "She was only a girl when it happened."

"Molly, aren't you being rather sexist? We were all the same age: twenty-six."

"But why for God's sake did you do it?"

"Why did *he* do it?"

When Molly doesn't answer—can't answer, she is gripping the receiver so hard—James says casually, "Look—why did *she* do it? Her behavior was all quite premeditated, I assure you. She was playing Hedda Gabler to the bitter end."

"Premeditated," Molly repeats slowly.

There is a long pause. Has James laid down the telephone at his end, or is he about to break the connection? There is no man Molly Marks loathes more than James McEwan but she does not—ah, does *not*—want him to break the connection.

"I really don't care to discuss the matter any longer," James says curtly. "As far as I'm concerned it's ancient history—ancient 'tragedy'—in which I have not, today, the slightest interest. I would be very surprised, indeed, if my brother had the slightest interest either."

"Yes. You're correct. Jonathan says he is through with it—he's through with it all." Molly pauses. "And he is through with me, I think."

"I doubt that!" James says cheerily. "He'd be more of a fool than I think him, if he broke off with you—too."

It has been some days since Molly and Jonathan last spoke: since Jonathan walked out of the restaurant. Molly has been preparing to move to another, smaller apartment, closer to the Foundation headquarters, searching through advertisements for rentals with alternating energy and fatigue, making the usual telephone calls—all the while thinking, *This* is the place I belong in, why am I moving away? What has happened, to force me away?

"But I called, dear Molly, to see if something can't be worked out between you and me, after all," James says warmly. "What do we care about Jonathan—let alone that poor deluded girl of a decade past. I do admit I've been, shall we say, aggressive in pursuing you, of late—but meant nothing by it. I mean—no harm to you." He pauses. "—No threat to your *literal* well-being."

"As to Danton's?"

"Ah! Danton! Well—" Again James pauses. Molly tries to envision his face, his expression—but sees, instead, Jonathan's face, Jonathan hunched toward her staring at her with his narrowed damp eyes, his forehead creased in strain. "—I hope you weren't offended by my little joke, Molly," James says. "That wasn't Danton's heart, *of course*—you know how fond I am of the creature. It was just a—tidbit from the local butcher's. A joke I'd thought you might appreciate, being the kind of girl you are."

"And no threat was intended?—'literally'?"

" 'Literally,' 'poetically,'—who can say? You must interpret such signs as you wish, Molly Marks."

Molly says softly, "You are the devil—aren't you?"

James laughs. "Alas, there *is* no devil. Just people like you and me. And Jonathan."

Molly says nothing; Molly feels her blood beating hard, hard, bitter and resolved; she does have the gun after all—she *is* invulnerable if she so wishes. James says, "Let's meet one more time, Molly, and talk things through *sincerely.* You have cheated me of certain comforts and you know it. The love-bond between us, the bond of Eros, has not yet been broken. If you decide, after our meeting, that you truly do not want to see me again, I will respect your wishes. I give you my word."

"Where would we meet?" Molly asks. "Not in New York. And not here."

"I have in mind somewhere quiet, even isolated—intensely romantic."

"Where?"

"Has Jonathan ever taken you to our old summer house in Narragansett, on the Sound?"

"No. He said it had been sold."

"Of course it hasn't been sold—it belongs jointly to Jonathan and me. Our father left it to us in his will. Not knowing, perhaps, that the house has romantic memories for us both."

"What do you mean? —Did you take Sandra Shearer there?"

"Dear Molly, there *are* other young women in the world, in my world at least, apart from that *idée fixe* of yours. Believe me! So Jonathan never took you there?"

"No."

"Excellent. *I* will take you. I will meet you there—that might be most convenient. This Saturday perhaps?—midafternoon? I'll arrive earlier and see to it that things are in working order. We do have a caretaker, so the house should be in decent condition. And the beach, the Sound—you'll see, Molly, it's perfectly idyllic."

"And if I don't come?"

"What do you mean?—you said you were coming."

"I didn't exactly—"

"Ah but you *will* come, Molly. You really must stop playing these games with me. This weekend will be our honeymoon at last—James and Molly—and Jonathan *not* a presence, for once. Nothing will happen to you that isn't an expression of your own deepest desire. I promise."

Molly surprises herself by laughing, harshly. "You didn't answer my question, James."

"If you don't come?—if you snub me? Well—that, then, you might regret," James says thoughtfully. "Not that I am threatening you, Molly—not that I hold up to you the example of Danton—which *was*, as you know only a bit of theatrical show. Please don't misunderstand. I never threaten; I never coerce. But you might regret snubbing me—that's so."

"Yes," says Molly, evenly, "I suppose I might."

50

Mrs. Shearer spoke of it as a kind of play-acting—you don't know how serious, how permanent, it is. But Molly Marks thinks *Yes I do know*.

51 Molly is, Molly is not—*is* going to meet James McEwan as he has requested.

Has she any choice?

If the man is mad, or even, in his cunning, pretending to be mad—has she any choice?

She examines the little pearl-handled revolver; weighs it in her hand. It does look rather like a toy—except for its weight. The boy who sold it to her said several times that it was "lethal if intelligently fired; as close up as you can get." It would not, he said, be "absolutely accurate" at a distance.

He'd loaded it, he said, with hollow-point bullets—"dum-dums" as they're known in the trade—designed to expand on contact in order to inflict "maximum damage."

Molly reasons she will have no trouble getting close.

52 Molly Marks drives to Narragansett in a strange wayward exhilarated mood—on the verge of tears one moment, laughter the next. The day is very bright; chilly; wind-whipped—it suits her soul, she thinks. She might be embarked upon a honeymoon of the old sort, a fairy-tale honeymoon, where you don't know what is going to happen because you've never done it before. But you do know you cannot turn back.

Partly because of the sunshine and partly for reasons of strategy Molly has chosen to wear her new sunglasses, whose lenses are tinted a deep mysterious blue. And her newly purchased suede jacket—fawn-colored, stylish, the kind of thing James would admire, *has* admired, on her. *Molly how flattering, Molly how chic. The perfect costume for every occasion.*

Since that evening, Molly has not seen or spoken with Jonathan McEwan. Perhaps he telephones her, or tries to—she isn't in the apartment very often, except to sleep; and, when she's there, she leaves the receiver off the hook. It's true she thinks obsessively of him as of a riddle; a fairy-tale riddle. She does not want to forgive him and she fears that, if it comes to that, she will forgive him. She will sacrifice Sandra Shearer to him—of course. As women invariably do.

And then, in weak moments, she thinks with a burst of childlike hope, Jonathan *is* good—he couldn't behave so cruelly, finally, to someone he loves.

As for James—Molly has not decided if she should give

the man time to greet her, touch her, kiss her; if she should risk, at the final moment, feeling sorry for him, or feeling her old perverse attraction for him. Or should she act with as much dispatch as possible, swiftly and pragmatically . . . ?

"It's self-defense, James," Molly says quietly. "Simple justice."

The drive to the Rhode Island shore is less than one hundred fifty miles—a distance almost too swiftly covered. Molly tries to concentrate solely on her driving, on the logistics of getting from Lindesfarne to Narragansett with the least possible difficulty. As always she finds herself hypnotized by the simple forward-motion of speed: that sense of freedom, exhilaration, no one on earth knowing where you are at any given moment—what, in literal fact, you are doing.

She has brought along an overnight bag with very little in it, a prop of sorts. It is her shoulder bag that contains the pearl-handled gun: she has been carrying it there, accustomed to its weight, for weeks.

The white wings opening in her brain . . . but perhaps it is simply excitement, not madness after all; exhilaration, not fear.

She, unlike the other, will not succumb to despair; does not intend to be a sacrifice.

James's directions are characteristically precise: Molly has no difficulty finding the McEwans' cottage, at the end of a narrow sandy lane. Of course the house isn't a cottage but a large handsome New England saltbox overlooking the shore from a distance of perhaps thirty feet. So this is the place "jointly owned" by the McEwan twins, Molly thinks. And a romantic place it is.

The Atlantic is rough, white-capped, the wind so strong that when Molly gets out of the car her hair immediately flies about her head. The sun is so bright she squints even behind her tinted glasses. But it's bracing, the impact of the day, the smell of the water, the very look of the house—its six windows facing her, blank, winking with sunshine. Bright as a stage set, Molly thinks.

The property is clearly in a mild state of neglect: the black shutters need repainting, and repair; the shingled roof, the screened-in porch, the front steps—all need repair. But the house is substantial, the lot large and secluded, the view of the ocean magnificent. There is a three-car garage to the side, perpendicular with the front walk; there is a wind-weathered gazebo above the bluff. An expensive piece of land, Molly thinks, —and how sad, that it should be neglected. That its owners have had so little use for it.

The front door has been left ajar, as if it were summer. Molly calls out, "Hello? James? It's Molly—are you here?" When she steps inside, her heart pounding with excitement, the flood of adrenaline in her veins so powerful she can nearly taste it, she sees no one; hears nothing except a radio, turned down low, playing what sounds like pop-classical music. James does not seem to be in the house, or within earshot, but there is a large bouquet of flowers—narcissi, carnations, roses—starkly white and very beautiful—on a table in the entranceway.

And a card propped against the vase: *Molly love! If I'm not here when you arrive come join me on the beach. —J.*

Molly calls James's name another time. No answer. She sets her overnight bag down on a chair; walks cautiously into the living room. The floor, covered by a thin well-worn Oriental rug, creaks beneath her weight. The room is shot with brilliant sunlight so intense it nearly blinds; its windows, high, narrow, curtainless, are framed by louvered shutters to half their height. Through a high-arched doorway Molly sees a dining room table and a dozen chairs set haphazardly about it. The furniture is old, somewhat battered, but good. "Hello?" says Molly, her voice high-pitched. "No one here?" She is both disappointed and relieved.

Through a long horizontal window she can see the ocean, turbulent and white-capped, immense as the sky. The beach appears, from this angle, to be deserted—unless those are human figures a mile away, barely discernible.

Alone, Molly walks through the downstairs rooms of the house with a strange sense of authority. It *is* like a stage set—

such emptiness, openness. Like many summer houses the house is both idiosyncratic in certain details (of woodwork, wallpapering, decoration) yet generalized, even rather anonymous over all—as if a number of individuals, having lived in it for varying periods of time over the years, had worn it smooth and characterless.

But, in the kitchen, she sees a fresh stack of firewood near the door; in the refrigerator, there is a considerable supply of food and drink—as if for a celebration. "No," Molly says quickly, shutting the refrigerator door. She has hardened her heart and there is no turning back.

Dimly she recalls a dream of the night before—James approaching her in mock affection, speaking words she could not interpret, and she thought, or said aloud, *Now! now! now it will be over!*—and she drew the gun out of her purse and raised it aiming directly at James's face—or was it Jonathan's face—and pulled the trigger shutting her eyes against the man's look of horror. And the dream immediately dissolved; became one of the many dreams she'd had between patches of insomniac wakefulness.

Molly is about to go down to the beach to look for James when she hears a sound in the front room as of a window creaking in the wind, or footsteps. "James? Is that you—?" she calls. Trembling, she goes to the doorway; sees, of all things, a white cat in the living room, crouched and peering at her—a neighbor's cat presumably, that must have slipped inside while the door was ajar. The animal is a small cat, probably not a year old, very white, silky white, with luminous green-gray eyes. "Kitty? What are you doing in here?" Molly says. "Are you trapped in here? Let me open this door to let you out."

The cat runs away, frightened of her. Molly leaves the front door ajar reasoning that it will have an opportunity to make its escape when she's gone.

Molly re-enters the kitchen, leaves the house by the rear door. The back of the property drops away abruptly and dramatically to the beach; there is a flight of wooden steps that looks slightly precarious. Here, the soil is sandy, pebble-strewn, overgrown with thistles. And the wind! The wind off the Atlantic! It very nearly takes Molly's breath away. She shades her eyes and sees, in the distance, two figures walking slowly along the beach—is one of them James? She wonders if there are neighbors here, at this time of year. She has not anticipated company—she feels a momentary sense of peril.

Apart from James McEwan no one knows she is here. Apart from James McEwan no one knows she *knows* James McEwan.

Self-defense, Molly thinks. She has no choice.

She stands at the top of the steps, shading her eyes, watching the figures approach. Until at last she can see who they are.

Jonathan, and James.

James, and Jonathan.

They have sighted her too: one of them begins to wave.

Molly whispers, *"No."*

Her first instinct is to turn and run. But it is too late—both men have seen her. So he knows, she thinks, transfixed. Jonathan knows.

Has she dreamt this too? Dreamt it, and forgotten?

Jonathan knows, then. James must have contacted him. To bring him here—to expose Molly—to destroy her.

Molly slips her hand into the shoulder bag, touches the gun. Its reassuring coolness, hardness. Toy-sized but lethal and it is loaded with six bullets and the safety catch is off.

As the men watch, Molly Marks in her suede jacket and dark flannel trousers begins to descend the steps, moving with care. There are approximately thirty steps and some of them are badly rotted. And the wind, the wind!—whipping her hair around her face, making her eyes water. It is a dangerous descent but Molly begins to feel buoyant, resolute; as if, at last, she were in the right place at the right time.

She is acutely aware of the men staring at her—the one on the left (who must be James?) waving at her and calling something she can't hear, the one on the right (who must be Jonathan?) walking dazedly as if the wet sand pulled at his feet.

But the man on the left is wearing a beige sweater like the one Molly bought Jonathan for his birthday. The man on the right has raised his hand too in some sort of greeting—or is it a warning?

Molly waits for them at the foot of the steps, breathing quickly and shallowly. Thinking, It will all be over soon, in any case.

Thinking, I will kill him just the same. And free Jonathan.

One of the men is running toward Molly; the other begins to run too, and overtakes him. Tall heavy-headed men, broad-shouldered, with dark hair: identical-appearing, or—are they in fact identical? Molly has never seen the men together before and has never before experienced this visceral shock, a dread powerful as a kick in the belly. She recalls the fear of twins, in primitive cultures; the superstitions about twins—that one, or both, should be killed at birth. How can such creatures be told apart? How, without their cooperation and consent?

Molly hears her name called. The man on the left? The man on the right? Now they are close enough, she can see they are indistinguishable—unless the one on the right *is* Jonathan, his cheeks even thinner than she recalls. But it is the one on the left who is wearing the beige sweater.

One is shouting: "Molly—he told me everything! Molly—it's all right!" And then, as if it were an afterthought, "I'm Jonathan, Molly—"

But the other cries angrily, "Molly, for God's sake—*I'm* Jonathan. Don't listen to—"

"—I'm Jonathan," says the first, his face contorted in fury, or pain, "—Don't listen to him—it's his idea of a joke—"

"It's his idea of a joke—"

"Molly for God's sake—"

Molly stands frozen, staring. The man on the left is Jonathan—isn't he? Or is it the man on the right who is Jonathan?

The extraordinary thing is, when Molly looks at one of the men it seems to her obvious that he is Jonathan. And when she looks at the other man it seems to her obvious—incontestable—that *he* is Jonathan.

The white wings threatening to open in her brain . . . but

Molly is in control. She would laugh hysterically, it is so preposterous; so cruel. So logical.

"Stop," she says. "Both of you. *Don't come any closer.*"

So Molly Marks stands on the windswept beach at Narragansett, in early April of a year she has scarcely registered, unmoving, transfixed, her right hand hidden in her shoulder bag, waiting. She looks from one of her lovers to the other. From one to the other.